Changeling Press, LLC

ChangelingPress.com

Hellacious

J. Hali Steele

Hellacious

J. Hali Steele

ISBN: 978-1-60521-810-6

Publisher:
Changeling Press LLC
315 N. Centre St.
Martinsburg, WV 25404
ChangelingPress.com

Printed in the U.S.A.

Editor: Chrissie Henderson
Cover Artist: Bryan Keller

The individual stories in this anthology have been previously released in E-Book format.

Table of Contents

Prologue

Momma had a wicked sense of humor. Said she named us after three of Daddy's better traits -- Sly, Slick, and Wicked. She called us hellacious sons-of-bitches and Sathariel was the demonic surname she tagged us with in his honor.

We're the sons of Lucifer himself, and since our mother is human, we're permitted above, as are other unimportant demons who wreaked havoc on Earth and its inhabitants. It's in our blood to take absolute advantage of every glorious moment, even though a blast furnace of heat follows us everywhere. Still, nothing rivaled the fires of Hell. And unbeknownst to humans, cold is just as bad. Hell freezes over each time some asshole mutters the fateful words "When hell freezes over." Never lasts long, but it gets so fucking cold a demon's nuts could crack.

Guess God has a sense of humor, too.

Sly (Hellacious 1)

J. Hali Steele

Born of Hell, will he destroy the pure heart he desires?

Sly Sathariel possesses his father's genes, and on Earth he creates all sorts of havoc for humans, though he never takes a life. His father, Satan, reserves that power, yet not even he could keep Sly from the arms of the pure and spiritual woman representing the Tree of Life. She entangles him in her roots, pulling Sly in a direction his hellacious soul dare not follow.

Waverly Malkuth has a premonition no human should be privy to -- she witnessed her own death. It's tearing her apart, filling her with anger and thoughts of vengeance that go against the grain of everything she knows. Giving in to the malevolence growing in her heart carries her into the arms of a man who can only hurry her journey down the deadly path she follows.

Chapter One

Raucous music blared in the club, glasses clinked and people shouted over the din. Desire railed against Sly's rib cage. Desire to unleash what he truly was, strip himself bare of the make-believe human image he wore and let loose the beast that ruled him. The hellish creature wanted nothing more than to crawl between big thighs and screw the brains out of the vision of loveliness dancing alone not far from where he stood. Pale, thin women didn't excite Sly. He liked deep tanned, soft, curvaceous bodies with wide hips and ample breasts.

This one had it all.

Sly could barely contain himself as he watched her swivel and gyrate her ass in front of the stage where the DJ did his thing. Her raw scent, the smell of sweat and womanhood permeated the air, teasing his dick to a stiffness he couldn't control -- didn't want to control. Horns and hooves wanted to burst through his skin, fingers wanted to reach into the pussy he'd sniffed for far too long now. This wasn't the first time he'd seen her. She had been here each night he came to this particular club for the last month, and something about the woman kept drawing him back.

Oh, man, I want some.

Looking across the crowded bar, he caught his younger brother smiling.

Stay the fuck out of my head, Slick. This one's mine.

Sly, born minutes before Slick, could best him most of the time, run circles around him when need be. But the firstborn triplet wouldn't be so easily caught off guard. Sharpening his vision, careful not to let the red flames of Hell lick from his eyes, Sly searched the room for Wicked. He couldn't feel him, no telltale smell of fire and brimstone that often preceded the eldest. Wick took anything he wanted when they walked on Earth, and it usually turned out to be something or someone his younger siblings had their eye on. Wicked skated on thin ice with the power below each time he used humans then tossed them aside as if they were old shoes never to be worn again.

Except with their father's express permission, they didn't kill.

Disturbing the balance between good and evil wasn't allowed. What Wick left behind bordered on dead. Mere shells of men and women, afraid of their own shadows, bereft of the spark of life in their sad, vacant eyes. In that broken condition they held no appeal for Sly or others like him who slipped from below to cavort in their very own human playground. Wick was off somewhere, and if Sly knew his father, he'd concentrate all his energy in the older brother's direction. Thank God, because he wanted this woman for as long as she could take his heated passion.

The club floor rolled as the earth rumbled beneath his feet, electricity blinked out, and the music came to a grinding halt. *Shit.* A few screams from those scared of the dark, shuffling feet, and cries of dismay from patrons trying to find the door. Lights blinked before flashing bright, music churned slowly to life, drawing sighs and hesitant laughter from the crowd as most returned to their tables, and others back to the dance floor.

Humans didn't discern the small quake as a powerful warning to Sly.

"They don't know where you come from or what a jackass you are."

Sly spun around to see Wick's glare of menace. No smell, not a sound, he was just there. "Hey, I was only thanking..."

"Say it again." Wick's lips pulled into a sardonic grin, his eyes became red molten pools. "You know Daddy hates that."

"Shit! I was glad *as hell* you weren't here." Sly tilted his head as he stared at his older brother. "Since when doesn't the smell of brimstone precede you?"

"Since Pops thinks I deserve more freedom." Wicked winked. "He loosened his grip a little."

"Until the next time you fuck up."

His older brother shrugged. "You should try dipping your dick in something exciting now and then."

"You're a sick motherfucker."

Wick laughed. "I know."

Slick strode over and leaned toward Sly. "You want her that bad?" Three identical-looking men turned to watch the woman weave through tables on her way to the bar.

Short, dark waves hugged her scalp, darkly tanned mounds strained against the top of the little black dress. Brown eyes appeared unfazed by the mini quake Sly's father had rattled through the club in anger at his thanking...

"Sly!" Slick pulled him from his reverie.

"Sorry."

"Hmm, she is a pretty little thing." Wick's eyes no longer blazed red.

"She's not little." Each brother stood close to six-feet-five with coal-black hair, broad shoulders and lean, rippling muscles. There wasn't a woman on earth who could resist them when they turned on the charm. Their biggest attraction seemed to be their eyes. When

they weren't roiling with red heat, they were icy blue --
totally out of sync with what they were.

"Mother had blue eyes," whispered Slick.

"Shut up." They didn't move as she stopped a
few tables short of where they stood to talk to a young
man. Sly wanted to rip the dude's heart out.

I can almost taste that pussy.

Sly's chest swelled with air. He knew better than
to start a fight with Wick, but he couldn't help himself.
"Don't turn her into another of your playthings."

"Why not? Her pain is flagrant." He rubbed the
front of his trousers. "Makes my cock hard."

Sly didn't have the elder triplet's power but he
could hold his own. Combing minds in the room for
happy thoughts, he bundled them into an icy arrow,
and blasted his brother's heart. "Not this one." Sly sent
enough joyful noise into the devil's firstborn to attract
an avalanche of ice to the godly bliss he deposited
there. Cold scorched any demon, but it carried deadly
pain to Satan's sons who survived on daddy's heat.
Wicked's red eyes flashed blue for an instant.

As if nothing had happened, Wick slouched back
against the bar. *You're growing stronger.* He twisted
toward the bartender and ordered a drink. "Shot of
Rare Breed." The bartender returned and placed the
bourbon in front of Wick, who lifted the glass and
drained every drop before speaking. "Do that again,
Sly, I'll rip your cock and balls off and send them to the
frozen tundra of Neptune." Twisting back to face the
woman who continued to move in their direction, he
added, "She's damn short."

"Fuck you."

"You mean fuck her, right?"

"Are you talking to me?" Her voice was low,
void of feeling.

"My brother, Sly, wants to fuck your brains out."

"For hell's sake, Wick." Sly jerked toward the woman. "Forgive my brother, he's rude."

"Am I lying?"

Damn, Wick's right, her ache is palpable. Makes me hungry. Slick pawed his genitals.

Enough! He didn't need his younger brother's two cents.

Her brown eyes carried a wretchedness humans would miss. Sly and his brothers didn't. Her breasts rose up and down with each breath, and he couldn't decide if it was anger or excitement. Something else rested deep in her dark pupils. Pain, utter loneliness... and fear. All three attracted creatures like him; it empowered them. Sly had no wish to draw on her emotions. *Damnation.* He swore silently at his thought of foregoing the use of any powers or magic on the woman.

Wick leaned over and whispered, "Sly, you're a pussy."

Identical triplets, the brothers were best friends and practically inseparable. Someone always had your back. The downside, someone always fucked around in your head. "Go to hell, Wicked." Sly peered at her and wanted nothing more than to erase those shadows from her eyes, see the true woman beneath the hard veneer she presented to the world. "He's not lying, but I would have come to that in a much different manner." He extended his hand. "I'm Sly Sathariel." Pointing out his brothers, he added, "Slick's the youngest, Wicked, the oldest."

Her small hand was cold, and empty laughter followed the smile curving full red lips as she stared at him. "Your brother is right, why not cut to the chase? Life is far too short, right?"

Who, or what, had caused such immense anguish, left her so damn wounded? A demon would have thrived on anger, sucked it from her, leaving her broken and without memory of ever feeling good or alive. Sly envisioned tearing the motherfucker limb from limb because the bastard who did this had not at least given her the solace of forgetfulness.

It wasn't one of us. Wick's words concerned him, but his brother should know, as he'd left far too many shells of life in his wake. Who or what else could make a human feel so… so lost and hopeless?

"Can I buy you a drink?"

"I've had enough, but you can take me to your place."

Slick pushed into his thoughts. *She's afraid to go home.* If his younger brother felt it, the power must be really great. Slick possessed his brother's abilities, but not to their degree. And the bastard was just too damn good.

Sly couldn't take the cacophony battering his mind. *Stop, both of you.* Monitoring Slick and Wicked took too much energy to concentrate, and everything they said he already knew. Her soul swirled with anger. She wanted to strike out, hurt someone.

He'd be her whipping boy. "You're sure?" Sly sniffed the air. She didn't notice because her brown gaze was glued to the front of his slacks. His swollen dick throbbed in anticipation of filling her pussy. The blatant fury, the anger blazing toward him, excited the demon inside, pulling it damn close to the surface.

Licking her lips, she swept a stray lock of hair from her face. "No strings?"

"No strings, no bullshit." Without turning to his brothers, Sly said, "Catch you guys later." He took her arm and guided her to the front door.

Mom would be proud.

Go fuck yourself, Wick.

Think I'll pay Pops a visit.

Sly went weak in the knees but caught himself by grabbing the doorjamb.

She asked, "Are you okay?"

Never had he experienced Wick this afraid of anything, and he no longer felt his brothers' essence, nor could he enter their minds. They'd already reached the bowels of Hell.

"Yeah, just tripped." She'd shone a glimpse of genuine emotion and the air grew cold around Sly. "You never told me your name."

"Waverly... Waverly Malkuth."

Beautiful brown eyes gazed at him, touched his very soul. Sly exercised every ounce of control he could muster to remain still. Did she hear air expel from his lungs? If her surname was to be believed, he was exiting the bar with an integral part of the Tree of Life -- and somehow, she didn't know.

Son-of-a-fucking-bitch!

* * *

The loft had its own elevator, and it encompassed the entire thirteenth floor. Waverly stood in a spacious living room containing pricey antiques, four other doors, and another larger elevator that made a whirring noise before bumping to a stop. She waited, but the doors never opened. Sly ignored the sound, so Wave continued to examine her surroundings. Somewhat at odds with the old-world décor was a very modern entertainment center, topped by the biggest television she'd ever laid eyes on. A very large, dark red leather sofa facing the wall of windows looked comfortable. Maybe he'd allow her to crash there tonight.

Waverly Malkuth was afraid to go home.

Every night, for the last month, scenes of her death played out on the wall as though it were a moving picture show. Blood seeped through paint, stained her beautiful old wood when it dripped to the floor.

Each morning, it was gone.

The only time she'd shared her horror, the man she'd brought to her apartment after a date laughed, swore he saw no stains even when Waverly pointed them out by tracing the dried brown stripes with trembling fingers.

He had his drink and left, calling her a crazy, whacked bitch for wasting his time. Wave saw them but no one else could. She believed the man who had picked her up in the bar would hear screams of death, see the blood if they went to her place for sex. But tonight Waverly was in his home, and a hard driving fuck was what she planned to use him for.

It was the only way to forget for a little while.

"Would you like a drink?"

Wave walked to where he stood in front of a half moon-shaped bar separating the kitchen and main room. "Later."

Never had she been this anxious to be with a man.

She stroked the engorged cock she'd eyed earlier, trembling at the warmth beneath her hand. Usually, she settled for what amounted to a quickie, and spent the rest of the night conning her conquest into allowing her to spend the evening at his place.

If she took him to hers, Waverly did whatever necessary to keep him there because it staved off the bloody picture show.

The gorgeous specimen in front of her blipped on her radar weeks ago. Something about him, how he looked and carried himself as though he owned the world. Sly Sathariel had the same chiseled, dark, good looks and black, styled hair his brothers did. Broad shoulders, narrow hips, and long, muscular legs completed the finest packaging of manhood she'd ever seen. Funny, they had the same eyes, but, in the end, Sly's captured her.

Ice-blue -- and burning with the fires of Hell.

If any sense at all remained in her head, Wave would run as if chased by the devil himself. However, she understood beyond any doubt, she needed Sly Sathariel, not his brothers, to end the grisly picture show forever.

Never had Waverly been so afraid.

"You don't waste time." The sexy grin stirred an unfamiliar feeling in her heart.

She shook her head to clear it, to jog her mind into remembering why she stood where she did. "I don't have much time." Unzipping his pants, breath hitched in her throat when his cock dropped into view. "Uhh… umm…" Words couldn't describe the length and thickness of Sly's erection, or the heat it generated in her hand.

"Don't stop now, sweetheart." He used his hands to push Wave to her knees. "Isn't this what you wanted?"

No. Her mind said *Stop, walk away*. Yet, listening to the logical voice in her head meant the horror would never end. "Yes." Wave's heart clamored for her to stay, to take what he offered.

Pre-cum spurted enticingly from the tip, slipping over the broad crown. Swiping it with her tongue, she savored the taste. *Sweet*. Wave stopped after drawing just the cap into her mouth, licked, sucked, and nibbled the ridge surrounding his cock's head. Deep throating Sly's dick, making him come, became her greatest desire.

"Damn, honey, you know how to suck cock."

He'd never know his was the only one she'd enjoyed this damn much.

Continuing to move her head back and forth, Waverly took inch after inch, in, out, constricting throat muscles to squeeze the cap. She released him and murmured, "I didn't think you'd taste so fucking good."

"You'll taste a lot if you keep doing that."

She gripped his ass, the other hand she moved to tug his balls from his pants.

He helped by easing his slacks down a little. "Squeeze my nuts. Do it hard." Massaging, scratching his sac with her fingernails made him bump another inch of cock into Waverly's mouth. Grabbing a handful of hair, he manipulated her head back and forth on his length, fed her more and more hard cock. "Shit, I'm gonna come in your mouth."

Waverly quickened her pulls on his dick. Bobbing up and down, twisting her head, she mouthed all of him as she fondled his balls.

"Aww, shit, take it," he roared as a stream of warm, musky cream splashed her throat. "Swallow it, baby, taste all of me." He pumped his hips, driving his cock deep as he got off in her mouth. "Fuck!" Finished, Sly reached down, gripped her shoulders, and brought Wave to her feet. "Damn, you're really something."

When he hugged her close, his heart beat an erratic rhythm. It shook Waverly to her core when she felt her heart match his as it pounded against her rib cage.

Too late to end it now.

Gathering herself, Waverly said, "I drink gin, straight up."

"The lady doesn't play when she drinks." He eased her from his arms and Sly's smile sent her into a tailspin. His eyes, those cool ice-blue eyes, seemed to look straight into her soul. The way his expensive silk tee molded itself around lean muscles covering his abdomen sent a twinge of desire to the apex of her thighs, causing her to suck in a draft of air. Wave hadn't felt anything like that in a long time, and she didn't like it. Her purpose here required maintaining total control of her mind and body.

The latter had become a lost cause -- he had taken control of her body.

Waverly decided on bluntness to regain ground. "Sly, right? Look, I don't play. I drink hard, and party hard." He stared into her eyes as she spoke. "And I fuck hard. Isn't that what *you* wanted?"

The man gazed at her another moment. Zipping his pants, he rounded the counter. Sly didn't make eye contact as he opened a bottle of gin and poured two drinks. As if to relieve tension, he rolled wide shoulders before he twisted and walked from behind the bar.

Using the time to check him out, Wave took in charcoal slacks that hung from slender hips, caressing his thighs like a second skin. Damn, without a wasted movement, he prowled like a lion, silent, and with deadly intent.

He reached her, handed a drink over, and then shrugged. "I wanted you. Whatever else comes with the package, I'm okay with it." He sat his glass down.

"You don't expect much, do you?"

"Not when I pick someone up in a bar."

Chapter Two

Anger made Waverly reckless. "Bastard. I could have left with any man I wanted."

Wave had had her eye on the triplets for nearly a month, but for some odd reason, the one in front of her stood out, and it was for him she kept returning to the club. They were identical, but she could tell him from the other two, though she'd have trouble telling them apart. Why Sly? Was it the way his eyes ate her up on each visit, made her heart beat faster, or the way he made her feel almost normal again? Unexpected was the desire he elicited from her body, and the way her vagina contracted when she looked into his eyes. The real reason she'd allowed herself to be picked up rammed into her mind, but Waverly ignored it.

"It's not too late. I can run you back over there."

She swung her balled fist and hit a brick wall in the guise of Sly's hand. He took Wave's fist to his mouth. Her heart lurched, and she fought back tears when he used his other hand to open clenched fingers and kiss the tip of each one. "Honey, relax, I don't know who or what hurt you, but it wasn't me."

"I…" Words clogged in her throat.

"I'll say it again. I. Wanted. You." Warm lips pressed against her knuckles. Releasing her hand, he grabbed his glass and took a sip. "I won't beg you to stay." Grabbing a stack of mail from the bar, he pivoted and walked back through the kitchen and disappeared into a room on the right.

Somehow, Waverly had managed not to drop her drink. Tilting the glass, she swallowed the liquid in one gulp and waited for the comforting burn to hit the pit of her stomach. *Get your shit together*! When he returned, she asked, "Can I use your shower?"

"Come on." He walked her to the door left of the large kitchen and swung it open. His bedroom. Wave halted in the doorway and looked at a humongous round bed on a slightly raised platform dead center of the big room surrounded by plush, white wall-to-wall carpet containing an odd design of circles and lines in black. Thick red curtains hung from a frame circling the bed, and another floor to ceiling bank of windows encompassed a whole wall. He really liked the bloody color.

He took her hand and pulled her into the room.

"You like red." She glanced out the window at nearby buildings.

"I do." His sexy grin enhanced his dark good looks. "Red is vibrant and full of fire."

"Aren't you afraid someone might watch you?"

"I have no desire to hide." Letting go of her hand, Sly traced a warm finger across her collarbone, sending a pulse of delight to her pussy, which released enough cream to wet her panties. "Nor do I wish to stem any voyeur's fantasy." Damn, his finger felt as if it grew hotter. "As my guest, you may close the curtains…" His hand cupped one breast. "Or let the world see how much pleasure you give me."

Two could play this game. "Or you, me, when they watch you eat my pussy."

"I accept your offer." He tilted her head up, brushing his lips lightly across hers. He planted a lingering kiss on the pulse below her ear, and then whispered, "I can't wait to shove my tongue in your cunt." Grasping her waist, he turned her to face a door. "Bathroom is through there and you'll find everything you need in its anteroom."

"Your bathroom has an anteroom?"

"It does." His light laughter relieved some tension.

Waverly opened the door, took two steps into the room, and stopped. "Can I sleep on your sofa tonight?" Shit, she felt like a scared child begging to crawl into her parents' bed. "Just one night?"

"You're welcome in my bed all night, and hell, I'm free the next night too." His blue eyes appeared darker, almost magenta. "When you decide to leave, I'll take you home and stay for as long as I need to be there."

Why had he chosen the words, *for as long as I need to be there*? "Sly, I'd like that, I mean, not you taking me home and staying, but me staying in your bed, staying here…" God, she'd made a mess of this.

The floor vibrated, and he reached for her. "Don't be afraid." Concern in his blue eyes as he searched hers appeared real. "It's an aftershock."

"I'm okay."

"Good. Can you run that sentence by me one more time?"

Laughter erupted from her mouth, shocking the shit out of her. Waverly hadn't laughed in a long, long time. It wasn't supposed to be like this. She couldn't possibly like him.

Entering the anteroom, she passed rows of linen, mostly red, but there were a few black, and white. A small open closet contained robes in various styles and lengths in shades of red, also interspersed with black and white.

Red, red, *red*!

Waverly was beginning to hate the color. It was everywhere she looked, but thankfully, it reminded her why she needed to be here. Entering the bathroom, she closed the door, walked to the mirror over the sink and stared at her reflection.

How long before the bastard flashed his red eyes in her direction?

* * *

Satan was going to roast his nuts.

Sly had taken a quick shower in the guest room, donned a pair of black cotton drawstring pants and a sleeveless tee in the same color. Sly stared out his window and thought over the last hour.

She had laughed out loud, and the space around Waverly lit up in a rainbow of colors. He'd wanted to reach into the air and grab handfuls of the brilliant shards glittering above her. Odd thing was -- Waverly couldn't see them, didn't know her happiness sent bursts of joy into the atmosphere, which latched onto anyone in her immediate vicinity.

Sly was immune. Shit, being the son of Satan meant always being happy. He wanted for nothing; riches, women, all the good things in life were within his grasp, he only had to ask, and it was his. Yes, Satan, Lucifer, whatever name people used, spoiled his boys to death. It kept them at his side. Was love involved? Sly thought so. After all, his father used to be an angel, and no matter what so-called Christians wanted to believe, God still loved the angel he had cast from Heaven into Hell. Why else would he exist? The lights in the kitchen blinked out, then sputtered back to life. "Sorry," he said. Such a slight disturbance surprised Sly, considering he continued to ignore the psychic energy attempting to drag him below.

He wouldn't get away with that much longer.

The door clicked open and Waverly entered the living room wearing a floor-length white robe. Hell and damnation, his cock slithered to life. "Damn, you're beautiful." Sly walked over, pulled her into his arms, and kissed her, lightly at first. Soon his tongue prodded for entrance to her mouth. Waverly opened, took him in as if he belonged there. Their tongues teased and danced together before searching sweet hidden corners. "I've wanted you since the minute I laid eyes on you."

"The bedroom," she whispered against his mouth.

He swept her up in his arms, then carried her into his room and sat her on the edge of his bed. "Tell me you want this or it won't happen."

"You already know."

"Tell me." What had transpired in the bathroom to take her smile back to cold and uncaring? Sly recognized it the minute she walked into the living room, felt it for sure when he kissed her. The fire was missing. He didn't give a shit. He could heat her up, but he wasn't going to touch her unless she asked for it.

"Sly, you know what I want."

"You want to be fucked, and it doesn't matter who does it." Hell, he'd lost his mind and any semblance of control. For some inexplicable reason, Sly was not going to be satisfied just fucking her. *Damn*.

"I left the club with you." Her eyes were cold.

"And as you told me earlier, you could have left with anyone."

She grabbed the front of his pants, tugging him closer. "I want this," she said as she rubbed the palm of her hand over his cock. She stared up at him. "No strings, no bullshit, right?"

She'd thrown his own words back in his face. He willed his cock not to respond, yet, even with his powers, he couldn't resist her touch. He gritted his teeth. "Damn you."

"I already am."

Sly dampened his temper and tried to understand. "Why do you believe that?"

"Evil haunts me every fucking night, the only way I can forget is… is… this." Waverly fondled his dick.

"Is that really all you want?" At least she knew what she wanted. Sly had no idea at all. He wanted her, but he didn't want to fuck her. He wanted something else, but damn if he knew what. How the hell had he become so confused? He also wondered how such a sweet, innocent creature with a lifeline to the Tree of Life could be so angry, so hungry for sex and nothing else.

"I'm broken, Sly. I'm not good for anything."

When she untied his pants and tugged them down, Sly didn't stop her. His semi-hard cock flopped out and bobbed in her face. It didn't take long for her to bring it to full erection. Wave's small hand pushed and pulled the skin back and forth before she ran her nails up and down the sensitive underside, making him weak in the knees. When she grasped his nuts, he lost the battle. "Want me to close the curtains before you suck it?" he asked as a spurt of cream pulsed from the slit and slipped over his crown.

"No, I don't care." Her tongue darted out and swiped the drop away. "It's almost hot," she murmured.

"Take it." Sly wanted to feel Waverly's mouth cover his dick and take him deep. "All of it."

She swallowed inch after inch, and he felt the tip touch the back of her throat. He watched as her cheeks sank in when she sucked hard, and then pulled back up his length. Wave kept her mouth tight until the thick ridge around the crown popped through her lips. Again, her head moved down, taking more this time. She swallowed, forcing her throat to constrict, to squeeze the head of Sly's dick. "Damn, honey, keep doing that."

Up, down, Wave bobbed her head as Sly fucked her mouth. Flexing his knees, he reached a quick rhythm of in, out, in again. Each time he drew out, her lips wrapped tighter around the base of his crown. Twisting her head back and forth sent a delicious twinge to his nuts. "If you don't stop, I *will* fill your mouth again." Waverly didn't stop. She sucked harder and faster, drawing continuous spurts of semen into her mouth. "No, no." Sly grabbed her shoulders, urged her from his dick. "I want to come inside you."

Kicking the pants from around his feet, he stepped back, and lifted her legs into the crook of his arms. "Damn, your cunt looks good." Sly grasped an ass cheek in each hand and lifted until he could breathe in the scent of her womanhood. He exerted very little strength to hold her butt off the bed, close to his mouth. "Spread your legs wide for me."

Wave obeyed him, and clenched a fistful of covers.

Dipping his head, Sly swiped his tongue through her pussy, and the taste of Waverly made him moan against her nether lips. He found her clit with his tongue, prodding it until she wiggled her ass in his hands.

"Oh, mmm, don't stop," she whimpered.

Sly stopped long enough to tell her, "Never, honey. This is my pussy now." Delving back, he licked, suckled her labia, and then jammed his tongue home. In, out, he tongued her cunt, swiped cream, thrust in again. Sly wanted to make her scream his name. "Say it! Tell me who owns this cunt."

"Sly, Sly, *Sly!*"

"That's right, baby." He watched emotion, desire, flit across her face as he continued to tongue-fuck her, and Hell's sake, not letting his true tongue swell and grow was the hardest thing he'd ever done in his life. He wanted to fill her with the demon's appendage and make her come.

"Fuck it, hard, harder." Waverly nibbled her bottom lip, thrashed her head side-to-side, but her brown eyes never opened, and Sly wanted to see them, to drive whatever horror she experienced from her mind, her heart, and soul.

His cock throbbed between his legs in readiness, pre-cum copiously wetting the tip. "Now, honey, I want my dick in your pussy." Lowering her ass until he could grip her thighs, he nudged the engorged head through her opening. Shallow strokes opened and prepared her for accepting every thick inch. "Take my cock, baby." Sly thrust all the way inside her, slowly, till his balls touched the crack of her ass. "Ahh, shit!" he shouted.

He began to move in, out, with long, rhythmic thrusts, each one touching deep inside Waverly. Over, and over, he took her, took everything he wanted. Her fists banged the mattress. She pressed hands into the covers, using them to leverage her ass up and down while her pussy contracted around his dick.

"Faster, harder." Wave's eyes remained shut as she gnawed at her lip.

"Waverly, look at me."

"No, no, I'm so close."

Sly stopped, and, shit, it hurt. "Look at me." Releasing her legs, his cock slipped out, and her feet hit the floor. He leaned over, bracing his hands beside her shoulders before kissing one eyelid then the other. "Open your eyes, honey?"

"Please, finish me, please…"

"Touch me, look at me." Hell's sake, he wanted nothing more than to thrust back in her pussy, come, and fill her cunt with his semen, but more than that, Sly wanted Waverly to see him. "See me, damn it."

"I'm afraid," she whispered.

"I'll never hurt you, baby." She opened her eyes, but did not look into his. Instead, she stared at his chest, and then raised her head toward it. Waverly moved her lips to the mark burned over his heart, and kissed it so damn softly. She traced the rough edges with her tongue. Her lips were warm, and the wet path she ran along the scar ignited his blood, sent it rushing to his already rock-hard dick. "You're making me crazy." *Fuck.* There was no way in creation he could explain the mark.

"It looks as if you were branded."

"It's nothing. A birthmark."

"A pentagram with the roman numerals one, two, and three burned into your chest *is* something, Sly. And why is the two circled?"

She'd run screaming like hell if he told her the truth, yet it ripped his heart apart to hide it. Why? He'd never before wanted to open up with anyone like he did with Waverly. How do you tell a person you know the devil exists because he's your father? Or that your mother asked dear old dad to mark you so she could tell her three sons apart when they were infants? "Hell and damnation, baby, give me a break." His engorged cock smacked against her belly. "What are you doing to me? Why do I want you so fucking much?"

Her head fell to the mattress, and she sighed. This time she did look at him. Waverly stared at him long and hard. "You will hurt me."

"Honey, you're mine now." Sly moved his mouth a breath away from hers and whispered, "I'll kill anyone who touches you." He captured her lips beneath his, sent his tongue slowly in search of sweetness he knew would be there. He tasted fear. Using his tongue, he swiped, licked, tangled with hers as if he could scour the fear from her mouth, her soul. Having had his fill, he nipped her bottom lip. "Don't be afraid of me, Waverly." He used a knee to spread her legs. He slowly pushed his cock deep inside her. Not hard and fast, but slow, deep strokes, and shit, it felt fucking good. And right, it felt so right to be inside Wave, loving her. "Forget everything except me and you, here, now."

"I can't help wanting you."

Whatever it was she needed to forget, Sly vowed to help her.

Her hips ground into his crotch each time he shoved inside her. "Unnhhh, yes," she moaned.

"That's it, baby, take what you want." His feet still planted on the floor, he reared back to nudge her legs up until her feet rested near the edge of the bed. Grasping her ass, he never slipped out or lost contact with her pelvis as he manipulated Wave's body until she rested in the middle of the mattress. Lying flat on her, Sly continued to grip her ass cheeks, held them tight, not allowing any movement while he repeatedly jammed his cock inside. His pounding became faster, more insistent, and Waverly met him stroke for stroke, grinding her hips, taking more cock with each invasion.

"Now, now, *now*," she yelled, gazing at him.

"Shit, shit." Sly wanted release, needed to come, but not until he felt her cream surround his dick. "Come on, honey, come for me."

"Sly, ooh, oh, oh… God, I'm com… coming!"

The bed rolled beneath them, sending him deeper into her pussy. "Aww, yeah, give it to me!" he shouted as he drove into her cunt hard. His orgasm tore from his nuts, racing to fill her with semen.

The force of Sly's ejaculation slamming into her vagina seemed to surprise her, and she cried, "God forgive me, but I want you." She glared at him in fear.

Sly couldn't wait for his dick to stop pulsing. He pulled his length from her, twisted and landed on his back, carrying her to lie on top. "Shh, baby, I got you." He pressed her head to his chest and breathed raggedly. *Shit*. Why the fuck was she so scared? "Talk to me, tell me who did this."

Waverly pushed up and stared into his eyes. "I'm afraid."

"Why?"

"I see you…" She hesitated. Waverly's throat worked, her mouth opened and closed. "You're going to kill me."

Sly watched a stream of tears course down her cheeks. "What the hell did you say?"

Chapter Three

Waverly Malkuth hadn't counted on wanting Sly, or enjoying his touch, the sound of his laughter, and how good it felt when he moved inside her. Nor did she count on feeling safe with him. How could she?

"It's you who kills me." Waverly wished he had proved her wrong because she wanted him more than she'd wanted any other man she'd taken to her bed. She thought he could make her forget, but not him, not Sly. The pictures of her dying were not always quite clear, but when she first laid eyes on him, Wave knew the truth. "The pictures on the wall… it's your eyes I see glaring red right before you murder me."

A dream, or a premonition, it didn't matter. Sly Sathariel would kill her. Every night she spent alone in her bed, she died over and over again at his hands.

He dumped her body unceremoniously onto the bed and jumped up. "You're out of your mind."

The vacant smile she'd confronted the world with over the last few weeks was back. Wave felt it in the terrible twist of her lips. "You'd like that, wouldn't you? Me being crazy?"

"I'm not sure what kind of pictures you see or what the hell goes on in your apartment, but I guarantee, neither me, nor anyone else, is going to kill you."

"God knows, I wish I could believe you."

The room shook violently.

"Waverly, you… damn, do you need to be so blasphemous?"

Her head cocked to the side. "Someone… something doesn't like it?" Now they could get to the point. Waverly had started to notice a month ago at the club, whenever the brothers were there, any uttered religious phrase brought about mini quakes and electrical disturbances. Her whole life she'd seen things others didn't, had hunches or forewarnings of local disasters that came true. Until she first spied the three men, she'd never had the premonition of her own death -- with moving pictures and all the blood and gore.

"No, *someone* doesn't like it."

"You?"

"Personally, sweetheart, I don't give a shit who you need to call on as long as you say Sly when I'm fucking you."

"Maybe you won't be fucking me."

"Get dressed; we're going to your place." He grabbed his slacks and shirt from the floor. "Hell knows, this bullshit is going to stop."

"The premonitions, I've always known about… there are evil things in this world."

He spun toward her. "What do you mean?"

She watched him stand deathly still. "You… you're evil. I think you're the devil."

"No, I mean what premonitions?"

"Fires, earthquakes, I know when people are going to die." She continued to stare at Sly. "Until something made me enter that damn club where I saw you and your brothers, I'd never seen my own death."

"Shit. Not now." He peered around the room as if he looked for someone.

The bed rocked and rolled, walls pulsed with life. "Goddamn it, Sly, what is going on?"

"Will you please trust me?" He gazed at her, took in every inch of her body as she sat in the middle of the mattress. "I don't want to leave you, but I have no choice."

"This can't be happening."

"Use my computer, password is satanssecondborn, look up Malkuth and every single thing you can find on it."

"My name?" Waverly pulled the covers around her knowing they would afford no protection from whatever rattled the building. "Sly, don't leave me, please!"

"I'm sorry." The floor split wide-open, fire leaped around the walls, danced over the glass, and a forked tail flicked from the flames touching the ceiling. "You won't be able to leave, but, I promise, Waverly, you'll be safe here." The tail dropped down, wrapped around Sly's bare waist, and snatched him into the breach.

"Jesus! God is good, God is great…" Waverly chanted and everything stopped moving; the bed, walls, and the heat from the flames dissipated. Sly's bedroom reverted to the way it was before the floor opened up and swallowed him. It was then Waverly figured out the odd markings on the carpet. "Holy fuck, it's a pentagram." Nothing she'd ever witnessed prepared her for this, yet somehow she understood; her life was irrevocably intertwined with Sly's. "Who, *what* the hell are you, Sly Sathariel?"

She had figured *that* out already.

Waverly jumped from the bed and ran into the anteroom to retrieve her clothes. After dressing quickly, she headed for the loft elevator. The smell of sulphur knocked Wave to her knees. When she backed up, the odor vanished. Pivoting, she went for the larger door. Same thing. The hideous smell surrounded her and sent another jag of sickness roiling through her stomach. "I'm trapped." She rushed to the bank of windows and peered out. Sly's last words rang through her mind.

You won't be able to leave, but, I promise, Waverly, you'll be safe here.

Outside, the world moved normally.

Wave peered below, watched cars ride up and down the main street, could see their taillights on the side roads. Buildings throughout the city held offices and apartments with fluorescent fixtures glowing from some, while others stood dark. Looking into the sky, stars twinkled and the moon shone brighter than ever before. She took a seat in the nearest chair and sleep crept up on her, but not before she thought about her premonition of death.

"They don't know," she whispered. People talked about the devil and Hell; did they know Satan truly existed?

She had just fucked him.

Waverly fought a losing battle to stay awake.

* * *

The devil, Lucifer, Satan, they were the same.

Sly Sathariel's father resided in a mansion appointed with every modern convenience invented. Expensive furnishings in various shades of red decorated his living area. Plush chairs, original artwork by artists who plied their trade so as not to roast in the ever-present flames, and a giant, wide screen television hung from the wall over an entertainment and computer center that would make a gamer salivate. Hell wasn't an ugly place, unless you burned there for unforgivably immoral sins. Having it as an address disturbed some of the lesser demons who believed they should remain above every damn day of their life.

With their powers, living on Earth was much more rewarding than cohabitating below.

Sly Sathariel, and his brothers, Slick and Wicked, didn't have that problem. They could live where they chose, until Daddy called them home. He'd made the mistake of ignoring Satan, and no one did that. Waverly had shocked the shit out of him with her revelation about premonitions, particularly the one where he killed her. Getting to her apartment and seeing what evil brewed there was paramount.

It's not as if the devil had any place to go.

"What the hell? Something needed my attention," he said as he magically fashioned a pair of jeans and a tee shirt to cover his nakedness. "I was coming."

"No shit." His father eyed him from a throne laden with jewels. "Why bother with clothes?" The material caught fire and cinders dropped at his feet, leaving him butt naked again. A few embers clung to the hair surrounding his cock, and Sly frantically brushed them away. He could take his father's heat, but this went too far. Satan laughed, the sound bounding through the bowels of Earth, shaking the ground it touched. "We've seen that tiny cock before."

"Come on!" He dressed in another outfit. "I really need to get back." This time his pants smoldered.

"Crawling back between Heaven's thighs and coming some more can wait."

"Did you do this to her?" Asking the wrong question, and in the wrong tone, got you tossed into the blackest hole existing in Hell for days on end. Sly held his breath.

"Son, I wouldn't touch her with a ten-foot pole." Red eyes glared at him.

"But you know who did?"

"Sit down."

His brothers, both of whom had stood by and watched Sly undergo a ridiculously mild punishment, scrambled for chairs as far away from Daddy as possible. This must be bad for his father to let him off so lightly. Tonight, Satan was sans horns and his tail as he nibbled nervously on a fingernail. Thank God, because when the leathery appendage flipped about, the damage could be irreparable.

Sly's seat tipped backward, slid across the polished wood floor, and flung him against the wall.

"Have you lost your mind bringing that name into my home?"

Righting the chair, he moved it back to the spot where it had stood, and sat down. "I'm sorry." A sideways glance at his brothers irked the shit out of Sly. They smiled at his predicament.

His father glared at him. "I won't argue that point since you're the sorriest ass in this room." He leaned back, his sigh whistling through the halls like the north wind. "Tell me how you came to meet the woman."

"At a club we frequent."

"Did you see her first, come on to her, or vice versa?"

"What the fuck difference does it make?" He knew he was pushing it, but the need to get to Waverly burned in his gut.

The red glare grew brighter, and tiny flames flickered in Satan's eyes. "Sly, if I didn't need you to help figure this shit out, your ass would be on lockdown for a year. Answer me, damn it."

"I watched her for a while, and… shit, wait, she did say she noticed us at the club."

Wick spoke up. "You jackass, didn't you think to tell me?"

"So you could take her?" Sly grew angrier by the moment at each delay.

"Shit, dude, I can fuck anybody I want." Wick tilted his head and studied him. "I'm your brother, you could have trusted me."

"Trust the motherfucker who's going to bury my cock and balls on a frozen planet?"

"Hell's sake, I was joking, man."

Sly glared at him. "I'm not laughing."

Wick ran a hand through his hair. "Sly, have you ever really wanted anyone I took?"

"No, but..."

"Fuck you, man, for not having a little faith in me."

"For crying out loud, both of you shut the hell up." The devil's words shook the walls.

"Now you've upset Father." Poor Slick, he didn't know when to stay out of harm's way.

"Goodbye, Slick." Satan flicked his fingers in the direction of Sly's youngest brother and he was gone. "Where was I?" When he stood, his clothes vanished, onyx horns sprouted from his head, curved talons sprung from his fingertips, and his long, deadly forked tail flipped out and slithered toward Sly. Grabbing the chair legs, it pulled him to his father's side. "Some force I can't grasp put her up to this. I've seen the pictures on the wall and she's right -- you're going to kill her, boy." His tail shoved the seat back to the exact spot it had occupied. "She sees you rip her throat out and tear her beating heart from her chest." Satan shook his head. "I'll say one thing, the little lady's got balls to climb in bed with your ass after what she's seen."

"She's not little." The crotch of Sly's pants heated up again. "Fuck me." He spat into his hand and pressed it against his zipper.

"Do you know where Slick is?" Electricity arced from the tips of his father's talons.

"No."

"One more wisecrack from your ass, you'll find out." Cloven hooves pounded the floor as Satan paced. "This shit is *not* going to happen."

"Can I do anything?" Wicked's gaze followed his father's tail closely. Sly wanted to laugh, but he had no desire to join Slick.

Red flames jumped from Satan's eyes and scorched everything within his vision. Everything except his sons. "I can't do this for you, Sly." Sadness erased the flames and turned his eyes black. "She's a child of the Lord, and I can't fucking touch her."

Sly laid his head back and huffed air from his mouth. "Then how can I?"

His father hunched his shoulders. "I don't know." He appeared to gain control as his horns, talons, and tail disappeared into his body. "If I'm right, anyone else from below who touches her will burn in Hell forever. Not even I have a say in that."

"So, she's mine?" It was stupid to be giddy with happiness, and ignoring the big picture. He grinned. "No one can touch her but me?"

The devil flopped onto his ornate throne and peered at Sly. "You truly want this woman that badly?"

"Yeah... Yes, I do want her, but I want her whole, and not afraid of me." He stared off not seeing anything. "I need her to want everything that I am." He looked at his father, then Wick. "What baffles the shit out of me is how she has no idea at all about her familial ties." Sly wasn't about to describe the rainbow of happiness that engulfed her when she truly laughed. "If she did what I asked before you snatched me home, Waverly will be enlightened."

"We know about the rainbow of happiness bullshit." Wicked stood and paced. "What does she know about us, and more precisely, you?"

Sly chuckled nervously. "She thinks I'm the devil."

All three men in the room erupted into laughter, breaking the maudlin mood for a minute. It wasn't long before his father readdressed the seriousness of the situation.

"Son, there's only one person in this universe I love more than you." Sly had seen his father's eyes mist over when he was a babe. That had been hundreds of years ago, and for the life of him, he could not remember why. "You don't need to remember that." Sadness permeated the area, and it felt like a living organism threatening to devour Sly. "That, I can remedy." Satan swept his hands upward.

Deep in the bowels of Hell, the gentle sound of rain falling on earth reached Sly's ears. "Father?"

"Go. I'll do what I can." He stood, crossed the room, and hugged his son. "True love comes but once. If this is yours, I will do nothing to stop you." He jerked around and returned to his seat. Gazing at his son, he said, "Know this, I will kill you if her premonition comes true."

Now the rain poured, slashed the earth. There would be mudslides and monsoons for humans to deal with. Sly understood it cleansed his father's heart of pain. And his father's maker would balance the catastrophe with love.

A fast moving, ice-cold blast of wind pulled Sly into its vortex and carried him back to his loft. "Son-of-a-bitch."

Chapter Four

Waverly believed in good and evil.

Earlier she'd witnessed something evil snatch Sly away and she vowed to fight it, and him, to stay alive. She had found Sly's office and logged onto the computer using his password. Typing satanssecondborn sent chills down her spine. She searched Malkuth and became engrossed in every word related to her surname. *Lord, The Tree of Life*! Things about using and being used, desires and needs, the Kingdom of God, too much to take it all in. It reminded her of a Bible book and verse she'd recited in church as a child. A time to be born and a time to die, a time to plant and uproot, kill and heal, all things she'd forgotten about over the last month.

One thing stuck -- Malkuth was the lowest part of the symbolic tree, which meant Waverly contained spirituality as well as darkness. How in hell had this remained a part of her thousands of years later? Only symbolism, she told her logical mind, but her heart and soul felt something entirely different as she read about God, and what he had made her.

It explained her psychic abilities.

"Waverly."

She spun in the chair to find Sly lounging against the doorjamb. "How long have you been there?"

"Long enough to know I want you and desire you more than ever."

She stood and walked to the window of his office to peer out at the lashing rain. "Want, desire, lust, they're words, Sly, words that all add up to sex." Wave couldn't look at him yet. She still needed to digest his disappearing into flames as well as what she'd retained from everything she'd read about the Tree of Life. "How did you know about Malkuth?"

"Wave, look at me."

She twisted around and placed her hip on the sill. "What will I see if I *really* look at you, Sly?"

"I'm not the devil."

"I've seen your eyes turn red with fire, and your brothers'. Tell me what you are."

"You've read about who you are. I'm not that much different." Ice-blue eyes caressed her, made her feel warm all over. "We both exist in," he gazed heavenward, "His world for a reason."

Shit, she'd learned she was full of darkness and evil. So what if spirituality mingled with her psyche? It was all mumbo jumbo and bullshit when faced with reality. If her premonition came true, this man, or whatever he was, would kill her. "I'm not sure I can do this." Yet she wanted nothing more than to rush into his arms. Sly had promised she'd be safe, and nothing, not even the awful premonitions, accosted her when she slept in his home.

He pushed from the doorway and pivoted to walk away.

"Sly, wait."

"No, you wait. I'm done playing this game." He glared at her. "What do you want, Waverly? A promise I won't kill you in some twisted dream?" He strode back in the room and pulled her into his arms.

She did nothing to stop him because she wanted to be there. Embraced, held, and made to feel safe.

"You don't understand."

"Come on." He grabbed her hand and practically dragged her to the service elevator.

"What the hell are you doing?"

"We're going to your place."

"No!" All the questions she wanted to ask, everything slipped her mind's grasp at the thought of entering her apartment. "No, I'm not going there."

"Yes, *we* are. I'll prove to you nothing will harm you while you're with me." The door slid up, revealing his sport coupe. "Get in or I'll put you in."

"How did your car get up here? We parked on the street." Anything to distract him.

"The building has a parking attendant." He opened the passenger door and said, "Put your ass in the seat, Waverly."

"You bastard." She climbed in and bumped her head. "Shit."

He had walked to the driver's side and got in. "That's what you get."

"Who the hell are you?"

He stared at her hard. "I'm Satan's second-born."

"Oh my…"

"If you say that name, my father will drop this car to the basement floor." He pushed a button on his key fob and the elevator groaned to life. He continued to look at her. "I think I fucking love you, and considering who and what you are, and what you already know, this… everything, can't shock you that damn much."

"You love me?"

"All the words I said, you latch on to those three? Jesus, woman…" The car slid sideways and bumped the wall. "Fuck me to tears, I'm sorry." It slid back to the center of the floor. "Please, nothing blasphemous."

"You're telling me I can't even pray for help?"

His eyes lit up. "Babe, come to think of it, you can pray to anyone you want."

"You just said…"

"I forgot to tell you, since your ancestry is tied in with Heaven, my father can scare the shit out of you, but he can't harm you." She watched his eyes go midnight-black. "In fact, if I hurt you, he'll kill me."

"Your father, I mean, Jesus, you really are the son of Lucifer." The elevator bumped the garage floor harder than normal, shaking Waverly up. "He can't harm me?"

"No, but he can rattle your teeth out of your head, so keep the heavenly father's name, as well as that of his minions, from passing your lips."

"What do you intend to do at my place?"

His sexy lips curved. "I intend to exorcise some demons." He feathered a finger down her cheek. "The rest is up to you, babe."

"You won't leave me alone, Sly?"

"If I can figure this out, I don't want to ever leave your side again."

If she were to believe what he said, Sly would die if her premonition came true. "Does Satan, er, your father, does he love you?"

He kept his eyes on the road, but he couldn't hide the telltale tightening of his jaw. "Very much." He glanced at her. "I can imagine what you think he might be like, but hell, I can't imagine having a better father."

"Your mother, she was human?"

"Yes. She's the one who requested the branding so she could tell us apart as kids. I think she loved us as best she could. Considering."

They pulled in front of her building. "How'd you know where I lived?"

"Shit, here we go." He got out and dashed around to open her door. "Wave, you'll have to get used to the fact I have a lot of magic and powers at my fingertips. They'll get stronger as I get older."

"Jesus fucking Christ."

"Hell's sake, woman!" He pulled the entrance door open.

"Nothing happened."

"I think it had to do with the way you strung that one together."

They reached the elevator, entered, and he pushed number three. Bracketing her head with his hands, Sly said, "I love your dirty mouth."

His lips crushed hers, and Waverly kissed him back. She should be scared shitless, should feel anything but the desire he ignited between her legs. She circled his waist with her arms, shoved her hips into his, and grinded against his hard-on. Their kiss was long, satisfying, and she ignored the fact that the doors had slid open. Their tongues warred, danced, tasted and teased until air became important.

She pulled away. "Sly, I have to breathe." Wave stepped from the elevator.

Dead center of the hall, he pulled her hand to his crotch. "We have to do something about this."

His engorged cock pressed against his slacks, twitched beneath her palm, and Waverly knew what she wanted to do with it. What if it was the last time? *Don't, don't think about it.* She had her key out. He took it and opened the door, but she was afraid to enter. "I can't."

He pushed the door wide, reaching in to turn on the light. "Nothing evil would dare touch you."

She peered up into his blue eyes. "But you can? Why?"

"Don't." He tugged her into the circle of his arms and kissed the top of her head. "I'll be right here with you, babe, remember that."

Waverly spun out of his arms. "My bedroom's this way." Her apartment was spacious and brightly-colored with pastels in blue, lavender, and soft yellow, all the shades she loved.

"What's the hurry?" His eyes darkened. "I hope like hell you're not planning to fuck me just to forget."

"I wanted to show you where it happens."

"Relax, honey."

She turned toward her kitchen and asked, "Hungry?"

"Could eat a horse."

She inspected him from head to toe, and then smiled. "You sure it's food you want?"

"It can wait." He grabbed her waist, shoving her back until her ass bumped the sofa. "No, you need to eat. I wouldn't want you to become the incredible shrinking woman."

"That's not likely to happen."

"Thank goodness."

"Is this where you say, I like my women healthy?"

"Nope, this is where I say if you didn't have that ass I would have never noticed you." He ripped her dress down the center. "I'll buy you another one."

He bent his head to capture a nipple through the lacy material of her bra. Moving to the other bud, he sucked until the cloth was wet. "Damn, your tits are hot." Sly used his teeth and ripped the thin covering away. "I want to see you." Stepping back, he said, "Take your panties off for me."

Waverly didn't know why, but anything this man asked for, she'd give it.

Except her life. That wasn't going to be a part of the bargain.

Somehow, she had to figure out how to stop the premonition from coming true.

In the meantime, she intended to live and enjoy everything he wanted to do to her.

* * *

Sly watched her slip the tiny thong off and toss it onto the sofa.

"I want to undress you." She reached for the hem of his shirt, pulled it up, and laughed. "Damn, I didn't realize until now how tall you are." Sly leaned down and placed a kiss on the tip of her nose before allowing her to stretch the shirt over his head.

The rainbow array of colors dancing around her naked body took his breath away. "Waverly, do you see the shards of colors evoked when you laugh?"

"Where?" She looked up, pivoted full circle, and asked him, "What do you mean?"

"Hell's sake, you're beautiful."

She gazed into his eyes and sucked air through her full lips. "Oh my God, I see them reflected in your eyes." She spun again looking for the vivid colors and almost fell when the floor shook. "You know what? I'm tired of your father's shit." She yelled into the open space of the room, "Bring it on, Pops, or back the fuck off."

"Don't play with fire, honey."

"You said he can't hurt me."

"I also said he could scare the shit out of you."

She grinned and touched what he called his birthmark. "Did it hurt?"

When her mouth touched the brand, he hissed in a draught of air. "Ssshit, lick it, honey." She ran her tongue around the pentagram, her lips covering his number two, and he loved it. "Mmm, that dirty mouth." Grasping the back of her head, Sly pulled her away. "Unzip my pants and take my dick out." He watched her small hands unbutton his slacks and pull the zipper down. "Touch it, baby." The coolness of her fingers enveloped his erection, and Sly thought he'd shoot his load in her hand. "Aww, yes," he whispered. Unable to bear it any longer, he made his pants vanish. "Honey, I can't wait."

"Go… goodness, you can make shit disappear?"

"Yes." He picked her up by the waist and sat her on the back of the sofa. "I want to eat your pussy." Dropping to his knees brought her cunt face-level. Sly eased two fingers through the damp folds. Finding her clit, he prodded it, rubbed it with his thumb as his fingers slipped easily inside her. "You want that?" Her body shuddered and he looked up. "You okay?" He pulled his hand back and rested them both on her thighs. Waited.

"I know it's you I see when… when, Sly… How can I need you like this? How can you turn me into a quivering mass?"

"Because I'll never hurt you." He planted a kiss on the inside of one thigh, and then the other. "I'd rip the heart out of anyone who touches you."

Her brown eyes gazed at him with more than lust. "Love me. Don't fuck me and make me forget, Sly. I want to keep every minute with you in my heart."

"Christ Almighty, Wave, I'm not letting you go, and you will remember this for the rest of your days." Realizing what he'd said, Sly remained motionless, waiting for the disturbance that never came.

Waverly ran fingers through his hair. "Maybe he's giving us this time in peace."

"Honey, if anything should happen, know that he's your greatest protector."

"Sly, I swear I won't let him hurt you." Goodness leaked from her pores, the beautiful scent permeating the room.

His heart wrenched and he silently cried to Hell and Heaven, to anyone who could hear him -- *she belongs to me*! Waverly, and everything good in her, wanted to protect the son of Satan, swore to keep him safe.

"Waverly…" Sly had no words for what he felt.

"Take me, love me, make me yours tonight."

He dipped his head between her legs, filled her pussy with his tongue. Her scent washed over him, engulfing him in her righteousness, and Sly never wanted to stop loving her. He licked through the creases, tasted all that she was, and wanted more. Pulling away, he stood and lifted her in his arms. "Bedroom?"

"Second door down the hall."

Sly strode down the hall, opened the door, and finding the light switch, he flipped it up. Lavender and soft purples covered the walls. A vary-colored glass lampshade topped the light on a nightstand beside the bed. He gently laid her on the covers, and then turned on the lamp. Walking back to the door, he hit the switch to turn off the bright overhead light.

"No!"

"Baby, it's okay." He walked back and eased onto the mattress. Sly pulled Wave so her ass rested against his dick. "I'm here." Giving her time to calm down, he asked, "What's in the other room?"

"My office. I work from home placing internet ads for a variety of news organizations."

"Has anything ever happened there?"

"No."

"Only here?" He wanted to get it out in the open, give her time to realize nothing would happen.

"Can't you see it on the wall right there?" She pointed over him.

Sly turned his head and scoured the wall with his extraordinary vision. Nothing.

"You don't see it." It was a statement, not a question. "If you did you wouldn't be breathing normally."

His heart ached for her. The smell of Waverly's fear filled his nostrils. "I'll hold you all night."

Her breaths slowed until she sighed. "I'm fine as long as you don't leave me." She nestled her ass into his crotch.

"Honey, unless you want me to take advantage of you, please do not wiggle that ass on me."

"Maybe I want you to take advantage of me."

Sly reached between her legs and pushed two fingers into her wet pussy. "Damn, you're wet."

"I want you now."

He played inside her cunt, stroked his fingers through the dampness until she moaned. Lifting her leg slightly, he nudged his cock at her entrance. "Wave, be sure, because once I start I won't stop."

"Sly, love me."

He slowly eased his cock into her pussy, and then moved his hand to the front where he could tease her clit. It wasn't long before they found a rhythm of push and pull that satisfied them both for a while. Sly felt her vagina contract, and at the same time, the crack of her ass clenched around the base of his dick. "You're squeezing my cock, baby." He continued to thrust in and out repeatedly. Needing more, he asked, "Sit on me, honey, let me work that pussy." She pulled away, and when the thick head of his dick plopped out, he damn near came.

Wave straddled him and used her hand to push his cock back inside her. "Mmm, yes." Leaning down, she covered his mouth with hers and kissed him softly. When she'd finished, she moved her lips to his brand, tracing the ridges of the scar with her tongue.

"Wave, Wave, don't stop." It was as if the mark connected to his nuts. Each swipe of her tongue sent an electric shock to his balls and made him jam his cock deeper. "Hell's sake, baby." Sly shoved his hips up harder, faster, each time she licked the mark. When her lips covered the spot holding the number two, he arched up sharply. "Fuck!" She leaned back, keeping her hands on his waist as she hiked up and down on his cock, taking every inch. Sly wanted to explode.

"Sly… unnhhh, God," she murmured.

His nuts ached with the need to come. "Yeah, take my cock, honey." His strokes sped up. He thrust in, out, over and over, loving the feel of her tight pussy, especially when she contracted the walls of her vagina. "Keep squeezing me like that, and I'll come and fill your sweet cunt."

"Yes, yes, yes…" She chanted the words. She leaned at an angle he knew let her rub her clit on him as he fucked her. "Ooohh, shit," Waverly moaned.

"You're ready, babe, come for me."

Her motion up and down grew slower, she leaned further forward and cried out, "Now, Sly, unnhhh… yes, oh, yes."

Back and forth, she slid on his dick, tearing an orgasm from his soul. "Here it comes, honey, ahh… awww, fuck, yeah, yeah!" he roared as cum burst from his cock and jetted into her pussy.

Her orgasm joined his, allowing his cock to slip in and out with ease. Sly tried to touch her soul. "Babe, I told you earlier I think I love you."

"You've changed your mind."

"No, but it was a lie."

Wave fell forward and rested on his chest. "Wouldn't expect anything else from a son of the devil."

"Smart ass. I don't think I do, I *know* I love you, Waverly."

"What are we going to do, Sly?"

"We're going to get a good night's sleep."

She rolled off him and snuggled her butt back into his crotch. "Promise me you won't leave."

"I won't leave you, babe." Sly wrapped his arm around her, pulling her closer. "I'll be right here."

Waverly sighed, and in minutes her breathing became shallow as sleep overcame her. Damn, she must have been tired.

Sly thought about how he'd get her below to meet his father.

You're not bringing her to my house and have his thunderbolts flying all over the fucking place.

Hell's sake, get out of my head.

You should be happy I waited until you were done. Satan chuckled. *I could have shown her a real cock.*

Dad, that's just nasty. Go away.

Son, be very careful. I love you.

"I know," Sly whispered into the night.

Chapter Five

"Sly!" Waverly yelled. Someone, something, watched her.

He slammed the bathroom door open and ran to the bed. "I'm here, honey, right here."

"Shh, they're in the room."

She caught movement out the corner of her eye, but before she could say another word, Sly glanced over and at the same time sent a flare of fire in its direction. Whoever -- or whatever -- yelped in pain and flopped to the floor. He grabbed the covers, twisted them, then flew to the corner, tossing the blanket over the writhing body.

The floor started to shake and Wave knew what -- who -- was coming this time. "Sly, don't you leave me!"

"Wave, don't move."

Hell no, she wasn't going to be left behind again. Jumping from the bed, Waverly ran to the two bodies huddled in the corner. When the floor split open and fire leaped out, a tail slithered in their direction and wrapped around them. "Holy shit!" she screamed, as a cold wind whipped into a vortex and sucked them to Hell.

"What the fuck is going on?" Satan reached the tangled mass of bodies and yanked the cover away. "I'll be a son-of-a-bitch! *You*!"

A tall, lithe blonde with ice-blue eyes scrambled to her feet. "Who in God's name did you expect?" She glared at the devil. "Jesus, maybe?"

"Ahh, you blasphemous bitch." He covered his ears.

Waverly held tight to Sly's waistband and remained behind him on the floor. Peering around his broad back, she spied his brothers standing by a door. *This can't be Hell.* The room, though decorated in mostly red, reeked of good taste. She whispered to Sly, "What's with you guys and red?"

"Why the hell did you latch onto me?" His voice carried in the moment of silence. "I told you to wait."

"Hell and damnation, I should cast all your asses into the eternal flames."

"Your father is, uhh, he's gorgeous, and wow, he's big!" Waverly hadn't expected the devil's home to be beautiful, and she sure didn't expect him to be the prettiest bastard she'd ever seen. Let's not talk about hung. *Oh my.* She glanced at Sly's crotch.

Lucifer glared in her direction. "Pretty?" He strode to an ornate chair resembling a throne. "Get up." Horns graced his skull, talons stretched from his fingers, and the tail, it whipped around knocking furniture about the room. "You are Malkuth?"

Shit, he'd read her mind!

Sly stood, pulling her up beside him. "I'll take her back."

"The hell you will." Satan's demonical appendages began to vanish one by one. "No one's leaving here until I get to the bottom of this shit." A long sigh whistled from his mouth, cold air blasting the room, echoing from the walls and beyond. Sitting on the seat, he closed his eyes, rested his head back, and said, "You boys remember your mother?"

A collective sigh tore through the space, sending glassware, some of the most beautiful artwork Wave had ever laid eyes on, chairs, everything not nailed down skittered about. *Holy fuck!*

The power gathered in this room could destroy the universe.

All three sons moved toward the blonde woman. Slick spoke first. "But how are you alive, and why didn't you let us know?"

Wicked leaned down and placed a kiss on her cheek. "Such beautiful eyes."

Wave's heart wrenched when tears spilled down the beautiful woman's cheeks. "I've been with you every minute of every day." She glared through tears at the man on the throne. "He wouldn't have let me near you if he'd known his father graced me with everlasting life."

"Fuck me." Satan gazed at the woman. "Josette, I would never keep you from your sons."

Sly was the first to hug her. He edged her away to look at her face. "Mother, what were you doing in Waverly's apartment?"

Blue eyes cast to the floor. "I needed to make her believe you would kill her."

"You gave her those horrible premonitions?"

"I gave her you."

"Damn you, Josette."

Wave watched her walk to stand in front of Lucifer. "I couldn't let you make them evil." She touched his hand. "I need them to hold one part of me in their hearts."

Never would she have thought the devil had any feelings of remorse, yet his red eyes grew misty and the sound of rain slashed against the place they occupied. She peered at Sly. "Is that why it rains on Earth?"

"Yes." He never took his attention from his mother. "You gave her to me? What do you mean?"

Josette pivoted toward Sly. "If she came to love you, even fearing you would kill her..."

Satan finished her sentence. "God would watch over you always." Red teardrops slipped from his eyes, and the sound of the storm worsened. "Josette, I never let them take a single life." He turned to stare at Wicked. "It's not been easy for me to control the three of them."

"When you let me go, I thought... I didn't know you'd love them as much as God loved you."

Taking Josette's hand, Satan drew it to his lips and kissed her fingertips. "Would it be that I was able to love you as I loved Him..." He reached behind her neck, pulled her close, and kissed each eyelid. "I never would have let you go."

Waverly's throat clogged with tears. How in hell could someone love a person so much, and then let them go? She glanced at Sly and his brothers who remained silent, seemingly mesmerized by their mother, and wondered if they were capable of the same thing. Could Sly walk away from her, leave her bereft as Josette appeared?

"No."

"You're reading my mind." She gazed into the eyes of the man beside her and wondered at how much he resembled his father, but had his mother's blue eyes.

"I wouldn't have left you even if she hadn't done what she did."

"Sly..."

"Waverly, I came back to that club each time to see you, to catch just a tiny bit of your scent to get me through the next hellacious day." He smiled at her and the rain stopped. "After seeing you, I never even thought of touching another woman, taking them in the way I've had you."

Uncaring about who watched, Wave put her arms around Sly, resting her head against his chest. "Though I believed you were evil, I felt in my heart you'd never harm me."

"No one, nothing in this universe will harm you." He picked her up and spun around the room with Waverly in his arms. "My own little piece of heaven."

* * *

After returning above to his loft, they showered together before Wave fell asleep in his arms. She needed rest after all she'd been through, and Sly didn't have the heart to disturb her. She slept in the safest place on Earth, watched over by Heaven and Hell.

Sly decided to slip out for a drink with his brothers. This time he used his devilish powers; no need to take his car as he'd never be bringing another woman home.

"Honeymoon over already?" Wick lounged against the bar.

"Don't hate because Heaven likes me a little bit." Sly watched Slick playing cards with the dude he had glamored so his old lady would get laid more. "Shit, she must have gotten it good today the way that bastard's winning." Slick had cursed the man with a spell that made him count the strokes when he fucked his woman, and he would win that much each time he played cards.

Wick eyed her dancing alone. "Gotta give the man credit. Her family's loaded, but he won't take a penny from them." He turned to look at his youngest brother at the card table. "I do believe if her boyfriend died, Slick would be all over that pussy."

"Shit, Wick, you just said something nice about somebody."

"Kiss my ass, Sly."

Sly's laughter caught Slick's attention. He folded his hand, and joined his brothers.

"Why don't you take her out to her pretty, shiny new SUV and get your cock sucked?" Nice didn't last long with Wick.

"Because I'm not the piece of shit you are." Slick ordered a beer, and then turned to Sly. "How's my little sister doing?"

"Waverly has a nice ass, and she's not..."

"Little," both brothers chimed in.

He chuckled. "Wave is just fine. She was pretty done in by all of this shit."

Slick swallowed some beer before saying, "Mom stayed below."

"Shit, see how long that lasts." Wick drained his glass of bourbon. "Heaven and Hell are like oil and water, the two always separate."

"She knows that, they both do." Sly ordered a gin straight-up. "A minute of happiness is better than none."

"Bullshit. Bartender, another bourbon." The drinks arrived and Wicked toasted his brothers. "Here's to being hellacious motherfuckers." He finished his drink in one gulp. Turning back to the room, he whistled. "Well, well, the ladies in blue are slumming tonight."

Sly glanced toward the door and watched as a group of nurses entered the bar. "Right up your alley. You like playing doctor."

"Sly, I want you to take a good look at the one closest to the door."

"Okay, what am I looking at?"

"My brother, *that's* a big bitch." Wicked's tongue darted out to moisten his lips, his eyes churning fire. "Catch you guys later." He walked toward the group of women.

"He's going to fuck her, and rape her mind."

Sly continued to peer at the group. He glanced at Slick. "Do you feel that?"

The youngest triplet concentrated hard. "Big brother is in for a surprise."

I'm good with it. Wicked took the nurse's hand and carried it to his lips. *Magnificent.*

She snatched her hand back. *Fuck off, pretty boy.*

Sly and Slick laughed until they doubled over. Wick had picked the only other person in the room with psychic abilities.

The triplets had a connection that only their father could break. It took more energy, but Wick used it now. *Slick, go to Hell. Sly, don't you have a curfew?*

"I think I will head home." Sly clapped his brother on the shoulder. "Tell Pops I love him."

Slick became lost in reverie watching the woman by the stage dancing alone. "Having no one to listen to the music with fucking sucks." He jerked toward Sly. "I'm happy for you, man."

"I love you too." Stopping everything for the barest of moments, Sly vanished. No one would remember he was there.

Reaching his loft, he smelled Waverly and followed her scent to a chair in front of the window.

"Hey, babe."

"Sly, would you do something for me?"

He leaned down and kissed her neck. "All you have to do is say it." He nipped her earlobe.

"Stop, I'm serious."

"So am I."

She stood and moved to look out the window. "I want to see you."

"I'm right here, Wave." Sly sat on the arm of the chair and waited.

She sucked in a loud draft of air and twisted around. "No, I want to *see* you."

"Ahh, you mean as I really am?"

"Yes, but… but you won't forget, and hurt me or anything?"

"What, and have Daddy roast my balls for eternity? Babe, you're stuck with me." Waverly stood with her back to the windows. "It's not like that, Wave, I change but I know every second who and what I am."

"Will you get larger all over?" He smiled at how her cheeks reddened. Sly didn't need to be in her mind to know what was coming next. "Will you look like your father?"

It wasn't nice to play with her, but he couldn't resist. He lifted his eyebrows. "I do believe you have a thing for Satan."

"Sly!"

"You did think he was pretty."

"Go to hell."

He curled his lip in a crooked smile. "Eww, Wave, he's my dad." Unable to carry it any further, he grabbed her hand and gazed at her. "What do you want me to do, honey?"

"Oooh, I knew you weren't jealous. You know I'd never have anyone but you."

"Damn straight."

She examined her nails. "It's just that, well, shit, his cock was huge."

"Sweetheart, mine is bigger." Lights in the loft flashed off, and then back on. "Okay, maybe not bigger, but damn near as big."

"What if…"

"I can control the size, honey." His clothes vanished and Sly let his body change. Eyes glared red as shiny black horns sprouted from his head, his chest broadened, and his feet became hooves. A leathery tail flipped out, stretched to its full length, and flapped around the room. Talons pushed from his fingers and grasped the flared head of his long, fat cock. "Look at me, baby." His demon's voice was deeper, gravely with lust and desire. Sly stroked his dick, squeezed drops of semen from the tip. "I'm the same man you loved last night."

Waverly released the breath she'd been holding in a whoosh. "Heaven above!" she exclaimed.

Sly smiled. "Sweetheart, Heaven has nothing to do with this." His spiked tail slithered around her waist, yanked her against his chest. "I smell your pussy." He gently tweaked a nipple. "You want to be fucked by a devil." His forked tongue flicked her ear. "I want to fuck an angel." The delicious scent of sex made his dick even harder. "You'll get everything you want -- and then some."

"I'm not an angel, Sly."

"Close enough."

"You're beautiful."

The floor shook beneath their feet.

"I didn't say… is he listening to us?"

"No, that was me." He planted a hot kiss on her neck before ripping her gown away. "I'm happy as all hell you're mine."

"Good thing you have money."

"Why?"

"I have a feeling I'm going to need a whole new wardrobe." She wrapped her arms around Sly and smiled up at him. "I know this little shoe store…"

"I don't give a shit." He pulled his horns in, his tail brushing around her waist before slowly vanishing into his body. Deadly talons became fingers again and Sly gently stroked them through her pussy lips. "I found a cunt I want to taste."

Laughter bubbled from Waverly, and rainbows of color reflected in the window as she gazed into his blue eyes. "God, I love you."

"Hell, I'm glad."

Slick (Hellacious 2)

J. Hali Steele

Slick Sathariel is Satan's third born, the youngest triplet. He keeps the peace and makes everyone happy but himself. Not anymore. Slick can't tell the woman he desires his family may be responsible for her lover's disappearance, or that he's the devil's son. But when he sets out to capture her for himself, his family's prying just might cause Slick to lose the one thing on Earth he truly wants.

Marcia Carter spent an hour in a handsome stranger's arms and she's regretted it every day since. She had been in the process of extricating herself from an unhappy affair when jealousy made her ex attempt rekindling their long-dead relationship. Now she's available, and the blue-eyed devil is pursuing her, but Marci is not about to share her millions, or her body, with another poor bastard. Yet getting him out of her mind won't be easy. Maybe one more time, one night...

Chapter One

Hellacious wasn't a thought that came to mind as Slick watched Wick observe the group of women doing yoga in the park's sandlot. His oldest brother was in a foul mood.

"At times she's all up in my head like a fucking London fog, thick, cloying, but I can't get to her." Wick shook his head. "Then there are the times I freefall into her psyche as if I tumbled from the sky without a parachute, and hell's sake, my cock roars to attention."

"I really don't give a shit about your cock, Wick."

Wick grunted. "Where's Sly?"

"Where he always is, stuck up Wave's ass." Slick gazed past Wick to the group and sighed. "I'm jealous as hell of the fucker."

"Not me. He's pussy-whipped and I'm never going there."

"Jealousy is an ugly monster, my sons."

Slick jerked around, surprised as hell his mother had crept up on them.

"I do not creep, Slick."

"Oil and water didn't mix again, huh?" Wick peered at their mother, Josette. "How do you deal with loving the devil?" Satan was not an easy man to live with. Hearing a burst of laughter, Wick twisted back to the women. "Looky, looky, Slick."

Slick watched the new arrival take off her sweatshirt, then carefully fold and lay it beside the pile of clothing and wraps already strewn about. He'd joined his brother at the park because Wick wanted to keep his eye on the nurse he'd had the run-in with at the club, but Slick never expected *her* to show up.

"I can't watch this," he groaned.

The woman from the club, the one whose legs he had spent a glorious hour between in an SUV, the one he desperately wanted... yet he'd given her boyfriend the key to her heart... and her pussy. *Damn it.* Last thing he needed was to watch her bend, stretch, and sweat. Her scent already reached his nostrils. Any more and his dick could double as a flagpole. "What. An. Ass."

His brother laughed. "And it's free now."

"What! When?"

"Easy, man. I was going to tell you." Slick wondered, only briefly, why his older brother glanced at their mother. "You wished he was gone, right?" Wick shrugged. "Maybe he's dead. Do you really give a shit?"

Slick glared at his older brother. "Yeah, like when Hell froze over you would tell me. Bastard, what did you do?" The sand shifted beneath his feet, grew icy-cold, causing him to levitate a few inches. "Fuck me." Uttering the words "Hell froze over" would keep his father's walls glacier-thick with ice for a few hours.

Genuine laughter bubbled from his mother's lips, evidence she liked what her baby boy had done. "I'm borrowing your brother, and please, don't irritate your father, Slick. I left him rather happy."

"That'll be short-lived." Wicked stared at Josette hard.

"Wick, don't be cynical. We must go." She twisted toward Slick. "Enjoy yourself, baby."

He barely heard her as he ogled the woman touching her toes. "Aww, shit!"

"Slick?"

"Hmm."

"We're leaving."

He let his feet touch the sand before looking at his mother. "Uh-huh, goodbye."

His mother touched his shoulder. "Look at me."

"Unless you want to see me with a raging hard-on, go already." Slick hadn't been with anyone for a long time and he felt as if he could come just watching the woman he'd wanted for a long time now. Wicked laughed and vanished into thin air, but his mother remained. *What the fuck!* "Mom?" Slick finally gained enough control over his cock to pay attention.

"Things aren't always what they seem."

"Yeah, yeah, right." He didn't want to let the brown-skinned beauty out of sight for long. Shit, if she bent over again, he would come in his pants. "I got it."

"Sometimes love must be lost before it can be found again."

If he didn't listen to Josette, she wouldn't leave. "Who's thinking about love? I'm looking to…" Hell's sake, this was his mother. "I understand, and I'll see you later." He had no idea what she had been saying. Figuring she'd leave, he pivoted back to the yoga group and forgot all about her.

This time he zeroed in on the woman's luscious tits and envisioned taut nipples in his mouth. Squeezing his cock through the thick denim material, he moaned when he felt drops of pre-cum ease from the slit. "Ahh, stay like that, sweetheart, stay right there." In his mind, Slick moved behind her, pulled her bottoms down, grabbed a handful of thick, brown hair, and slipped his big, hard cock right into her moist cunt.

"Poor baby!"

"For crying out loud!" Raucous laughter slammed into his brain. Wick and Sly. Bastards. He did the best he could to hide himself by twisting sideways. "Mom, go away!"

Horny fuck.

Screw you, Wick.

You should be ashamed, making mom witness your debauchery.

Sly, kiss my ass. You could have warned me.

"The look on your face was priceless."

Hearing Sly beside him, Slick turned and took a swing at him. Sly sidestepped and he flew from the trees to the edge beyond, and nose-dived into the sandlot not far from the group, which prepared to leave.

"Son-of-a-bitch," he hollered. "Goddamn it, does Wave know you're missing?"

The ground rumbled beneath him, sending a huge sand funnel into the air. When it sprayed back to earth, it covered every part of him but his face, and pinned him to the ground. "Give me a fucking break." Laying his head in the soft, warm sand, Slick gave up. "Sly, you'll pay for this."

Wasn't me, but don't do anything drastic. You got company.

"You okay?" He'd know the voice anywhere. "I'm Marcia... wait, I know you from the club."

"Uhh, hi." Hi, that's all he could come up with. Hell, she'd sucked his cock, he'd fucked her tight pussy good, and all he could come up with was hi. Damn.

"What are you doing?" She moved her hands to her waist. "Are you some kind of pervert, watching us from the trees?"

"No, uhh, I... I fell."

"Fell from where?" Marcia glared at him. "Buddy, we will kick your ass."

The nurse Wicked had an interest in arrived and peered at him. "Let's throw more sand on the jackass, keep him covered until we can get the police here."

"Wait, I can explain." He remained paralyzed beneath the sand.

No you can't. Wick's laughter coursed through his mind. *Look at the tits on Lori, man.*

His attention flew to the hard nubs on Wick's love interest. *You motherfucker.*

"Are you glaring at my breasts?"

"No, I'm not, Lori…"

"How the hell do you know my name?" She began to kick sand in his face.

He sputtered through the assault. "My brother…" Another scoop of sand momentarily blinded him.

"Did he talk about me?" She stopped and peered down at Slick. "He's a freaking nut job."

Bitch! His brother's anger heated the sand covering his body.

Wick, stop! Slick focused his eyes on Marcia. She was gorgeous in her fury. Big brown eyes pierced him, made his cock full all over again as her ample breasts rose and fell above him. Listening to him and Lori, she continued to glare. Marcia's skin glistened in the sun, made him wish he could lick and taste her all over once more. Suddenly, the sand moved, felt lighter, and his dick was on the rise. Shit! He had to put an end to this.

"Tell your brother to stay the hell away from me," Lori warned.

"Ladies." As they turned to look at the new arrival, air whooshed from Slick. It was his father in the guise of a gray-haired old man. For him to pay a visit to the topside meant some serious shit was about to jump off.

"Uhh…"

"I watched him fall from the trees where he was bird watching. Seems the youngster has a concussion or something." He held a pair of binoculars.

"Uhh…" *Bird watching, Dad, come on, some help here.* Before Satan appeared out of nowhere, Slick had intended to bring time to a standstill, extricate himself from his father's web.

"Hmm. He keeps saying the same thing."

Marcia looked concerned. "Lori, tell everyone to eat without me. I'll take him home." She stooped down. "Do you live around here?"

"You want me to come with you?" Lori's hands rested on her hips. "I don't trust these guys." She shook her head. "There's something weird about them."

Marcia smiled at her friend. "I'll call you later."

"Looks as if he'll be okay." His father patted Marcia's shoulder. "I'll leave him to you, miss, but be careful, you never know what these young men can get up to nowadays." The devil winked at his son and walked away.

Fuck.

Moving his hands, he began to dig himself from the sand. Pissed off did not even start to explain the anger roiling through his body. Every single member of his family had abandoned him, and it didn't sit well with Slick.

Didn't sit well at all.

* * *

Marci Carter had grown used to the best things in life, and held little to no respect for anyone who didn't go after what they wanted. At the very least, every man should hold a job. The last man she'd been involved with had one -- he played cards for a living.

Bastard was good in bed, *when* he got it up. He treated her well enough, and she liked him, but knew their relationship headed nowhere. He wouldn't change, and she didn't expect him to because he would have been right for someone, just not her. She'd been on her way to leaving the long-dead relationship behind when the guy sitting in her passenger seat dropped on the scene.

He was one third of the triplets every woman at the club had wet dreams over. Prettiest blue eyes she'd ever gazed into, and with a head full of gorgeous, wavy black hair. She'd seen him in the buff, remembered the six-pack that rested on his abdomen. And, whew, he had the biggest, sweetest cock she'd ever had or tasted. Her cheeks grew warm with color. Freaking guilt.

One night, after a few drinks too many, she had snared him for a glorious hour, and damn, he was good. Got under her skin, too. The only bad part of it was Marci felt guilty. After the bout of guilt came a bit of anger and she wanted to direct it at the man beside her.

That fateful night he whispered something to her then-boyfriend that lit a spark in him to rekindle the romance she was well on her way to ending. It lasted a little longer and, again, ended up going nowhere. It only managed to use up another few months of her life. Shoot, if he was still around, he'd probably be after her -- or her money. Oh, he did a great job of acting like he didn't want any of it, but if she offered, he never refused. The last time she saw him they argued over the card games, and he'd vanished that night. She hadn't heard from him since.

Good riddance.

She pulled to the curb of a high-rise that, when apartments became available, had a waiting list not even she could buy her way onto, and damn if she would ask her father for help. "You live here?"

"You got a problem with that?"

"Don't be a smart-ass. There is a police station around the corner full of cops who would love to lock up a peeping tom pervert."

"Look, sweetheart, I'm not a pervert."

"Right. You fell out of a tree bird watching." She squinted. "Where are your binoculars?"

"Uhh…"

"Jesus, do you say anything else?" The ground rumbled but it only lasted a few seconds. "Damn earthquakes are getting on my nerves."

"Don't get all churchy on me now calling for heavenly help and shit."

"Now! Why, you bastard." Her hand connected but not with his face. "What's that mean?"

He held her fist in a tight grip and peered at her. "I didn't mean anything." He grinned. "I'm just not the religious type."

Did the sun grow brighter when he smiled? "Well, watch what you say, I'm a little sensitive about the night we… well, when we did it."

"*Did* it?" He kissed the back of her hand and then let it go. "Marcia, I've thought of nothing else but doing it with you again."

"You never came on to me. Why?" What would she have done if he did?

"You liked your boyfriend, and I understand having a rough patch. Wasn't trying to interfere."

"And now?"

"Rumor has it he left you."

"Left me, my ass." Okay, so he had left her. "I'm all right with it."

"You sure?"

"Hey, there's a little of my day remaining, if you don't mind." She didn't want or need his pity.

"Want to come up?" She watched him press fingers to his temples. "I'm still a little dizzy."

"You can't do better than that?"

"Really, I need you -- your help." He stepped from the vehicle and motioned for the doorman. "See to her car, please." Leaning back down, he smiled. "I swear, you'll be safe with me." He put a hand on his chest. "I might have a concussion."

What could it hurt? Plus, she wanted to see inside. Leaving the car, she handed the keys over and glanced at him as he nudged her toward the building. Dang, he was hot. She decided if he lived here, he couldn't be all bad. At least he had a job, and a good one to afford this place.

The lobby was quiet with only a uniformed man at the desk who nodded. She peered up and gasped. "Beautiful." A hand-painted mural of angels covered the ceiling. One stood out because he had long, jet-black hair, a muscular torso with narrow hips, long athletic legs, and red eyes. It brought to mind the Bible stories about Satan being cast into Hell. Even with the red eyes, he was the most beautiful of all the figures. She glanced at Slick, back at the painting, and shook her head. Coincidence.

He stepped into the elevator, and she followed checking out his ass.

"You looking at my ass?"

"No."

"Liar."

"Well, shit, I remember it being a pretty nice ass."

"Pervert."

She laughed. Okay, he wasn't so bad.

The doors slid open on the twelfth floor. "You have the whole floor?" They stood in a penthouse-type vestibule decorated a little more modern than she cared for, though she liked the deep, red walls. "Nice," she murmured.

"Thanks. Come on." He grabbed her hand and tugged her to a door that opened before he touched it.

"Dude, thought you'd stay out today. I'm having company over."

"What the fuck, Wick." He pulled Marci behind him. "Don't mind my brother, he's leaving."

"Why the hell would I leave my place? You moved in with me after you got booted from your shanty."

"Wick, I'm not playing games with you."

His brother walked over to the window and looked down. Turning, he spoke to Marcia. "I'm Wicked, you are?"

"Marcia Carter."

"Well, Miss Carter, do you drive a red SUV?"

"Yes."

"Better hurry back down 'cause they're hooking it up. Why'd you park in a tow-a-way zone?"

She spun around to glare at Slick. "You live with your brother, and they're towing my car?"

"Look, I don't know what's going on here."

"I do. You think because my boyfriend left, you can get your grubby hands on me again." She tilted her head. "You weren't that good."

"Grubby hands?"

Wicked laughed. "Honey, you better hurry, they're about done."

Slick's footfalls sounded behind Marci.

"Wait!" He reached the elevator before the doors closed. "I'm sorry, I'm not sure what kind of game my brother is playing, but I'll straighten it out later." The doors whispered shut. "Please, believe me."

She stared into his eyes and, God, if asked, Marci would have said red sparks flickered in their depths. "I'm not interested in..." The lights blinked out, the elevator groaned and then dropped so fast she slipped to the floor. "No!" she yelled.

Slick reached down, pulled her into his arms. "Shh, I got you, it's okay."

She wrapped her arms around him. "Don't let me go." It was pitch-black.

"Never." He reached for her chin, lifted it, and somehow, he found her mouth.

Slick kissed her in the dark.

Marcia Carter had been kissed many times in her life, but never had she been kissed so well she forgot she was about to die in an elevator plunging twelve stories to the ground. His tongue tasted better than she remembered as he drove it into her mouth, touched every corner, filling her with lust. She tightened her hold around his waist, didn't want him to stop. The kiss was deep, satisfying and long... Slick held her and showed no mercy as he took what he wanted. Their hips bumped together, his knees dipped as he ground into her again, and again.

Breathless, coming to her senses, she opened her eyes, pushed him away and fell back against the wall. "Damn, what happened?" The doors were open and lights shone bright as she peered around him at the desk attendant who quickly looked down at a sheet of paper he held.

"We're fine. The lights went out."

"It would be a cold day in hell before I believed that." She glared at him and then walked out of the elevator.

"Ma'am?"

"What?" She hadn't meant to yell at the attendant. "I'm sorry."

He handed her the paper. "The tow company left this for you."

She turned to look at Slick, who seemed frozen to the spot where she'd left him. "Stay. The. Fuck. Away. From. Me." She released a long breath of air and twisted back to the attendant. "Could you call me a cab, please?"

Marcia Carter left the building hoping she'd seen the last of the blue-eyed devil who for one hour, months ago, had given her heaven.

Chapter Two

Slick's feet remained frozen where he stood in the elevator. "Enough already," he cried. Marci had uttered the words "cold day in hell." She may as well have said "till hell freezes over." The way his day was going, he knew the backlash would strike him.

And it had.

His father kept his feet planted to the floor, cold seeping through his bones and bringing with it stabs of pain. "Father, you can't keep me rooted here for the hour or so it'll take to thaw there."

I should drag your ass down here to suffer as we are.

"It's Wick's fault."

Control the young woman, or leave her alone.

That wasn't going to happen.

His body plunged out of the elevator doors, and they slammed shut. The young demon at the desk looked up in surprise. "Sir?"

"I'm good." Trying to appear in control, he walked to the stairway where he yanked the door open, and vanished to his apartment.

"You're back so soon?" Wick held a beer, and Sly sat across from him in Slick's favorite chair in front of the window.

"You motherfuckers have lost your minds." The seat Sly rested in violently tilted, tossing his brother across the room and into the wall. Turning to Wicked, he mentally flipped the beer Wick held upside down, pouring the frosty liquid into his lap.

He jumped up, glared at Slick, and burst out laughing. "Well, I'll be damned. You do have a set of balls." Waving his hand, he donned another pair of slacks. He turned to watch Sly right the chair. He wore a smile. "Can you believe little bro?"

"Love does funny shit to a person."

Wicked twisted toward him. "Just don't let this show of power go to your head."

Slick huffed out a lungful of air. "Why, man? Why?"

"Why what?"

"Don't play with me. This is the wrong time."

"You think you have a chance with her?"

"Yeah, I do."

"And if he comes back?"

"She says she's over him." Damn, when he'd asked if she was sure, Marcia had changed the subject.

"And don't be like Sly, making a promise to stay out of her mind."

"I won't need to read her mind. I can win her without that bullshit."

"Right, right." Wick's laughter dripped with sarcasm.

"I'm not going to delve into her psyche and root around like you would."

"What the fuck is it with you two?" He shook his head. "Women are most adept at telling lies."

"Whoa, man, don't bundle all women in a group like that. Wave would never lie." Sly glared at their eldest brother.

Wick pulled another frosty beer out of thin air, and sat back down in the same, magically dry, spot. "Your woman is different. She has," he glanced skyward, "ties above. She can't lie."

"She wouldn't lie if she didn't have a heavenly connection."

Slick needed to stop this before it got out of hand. After the last altercation between his two older brothers he'd spent more time than he cared to fixing his place. "Could you two take this somewhere else?"

Wicked spun on him. "Fuck off."

"Fuck off? This is my place. Skedaddle your ass to the fourteenth floor where you can do as you please."

"Skedaddle. What the hell kind of word is that?" Sly laughed.

Wick wasn't done. "You really think Waverly wouldn't lie to you if she could get away with it?"

"Hell's sake, Wick, let it go." Slick was thrown against the wall, and held pinned there. "What the…"

"Answer me, Sly."

"Bro, I don't know what your problem is, but it's not with Slick. Let him go."

"You gonna make me?"

Heat in the apartment blossomed a hundred degrees, and they groaned in unison, knowing what was coming. Slick fell to the floor as it split open. The flames licked through the space followed by Lucifer's forked tail. Flapping around, it destroyed every piece of furniture in the room before it wrapped around the triplets and yanked them through the flaming abyss, and below.

Slick brushed at the embers on his pants. "I didn't start this shit. Wick was in my apartment playing games."

"What is happening to each of you?"

"Each of you?" Wick flopped into a chair and eyed Sly. "I'm not the one pussy-whipped." Turning toward Slick, he added, "Or the one trying to wrangle a piece of ass."

"Wicked, what did crawl up your ass and die?"

Slick thought, for a change, he might come out of this unscathed.

"What the fuck do you mean?"

Holy shit! Slick watched as his brother's lips snapped shut forming a solid line, and his cheeks puffed out. His older brother's eyes turned red with fury, and horns sprouted only to melt into his hair.

"Don't you dare come into my house and act like you own it. I'm not your brother, and I will whip your ass from here to kingdom come and back." He and Sly watched silently as Satan's horns pulled back in his head, followed by the talons disappearing, and the tail flipping out of sight. He twisted and dropped onto his throne. "Christ, I'm tired."

A bolt of lightning blasted through the wall and wedged there. All eyes watched it wage war with the stone holding it. The shaft shook left, right, and then slid forward another foot.

Josette appeared from a white mist and stood, her back to the jagged bolt. "Lucifer, say you're sorry."

"The hell I will."

"Lucifer…"

"For crying out loud, I'm sorry, okay."

The bolt slid back through the wall and shook the earth as it left Hell and traveled heavenward.

"What in the world is going on?" She walked to Satan, caressed his cheek.

Slick watched his father gaze at his mother. "Brothers should never harm each other." Josette pressed a light kiss on his lips, and he leaned around her to look at Slick. His father winked. "Bye-bye, Slick."

Sucked from Hell, he hurtled back to his apartment. What was up with Satan winking at him, twice in one day, had his father lost his mind? And for the first time ever, he worried about Wicked, whose lips had remained stuck together before Slick left. The idea of returning and speaking on his brother's behalf flew out the window when he picked up Marci's lingering scent in his living room.

Grabbing his keys, Slick headed to the service elevator where his car sat. With all that transpired, he'd be at the club just after happy hour. He couldn't reach ground level fast enough, and the instant the doors opened, he revved the engine and skidded onto the main street. In front of the club, he slid sideways into a space, killed the engine, and jumped out. Looking up, then down the street, he spotted the red SUV.

Slick entered the door and didn't have to look hard to find Marcia. She loved to dance and, as usual, she shimmied her ass around the floor. The only problem, someone else rubbed against her big butt.

The man reached for his throat, coughing and gagging, then ran toward the men's room.

Taking his place, Slick prodded the DJ's mind to play a slow jam. "I like the way you move your ass," he whispered in her ear.

"You have balls as big as the Liberty Bell." She tried to pull from his embrace. "Slick, let me go."

"Not until you hear me out."

She settled down as he expertly maneuvered her through a few intricate dance steps, wrapping her back into his arms. "Damn, you smell good." He settled his hand on her ass. "Come to my place, and I swear, it's mine."

"Why would your brother play games with me?"

"Sweetheart, there's no accounting for Wicked's behavior sometimes."

"He owes me the tow fee."

"I'll make sure he pays it."

"Where is he now?"

Slick smiled over her head. "He'll be visiting my dad for a while."

"I'm not sure…"

He leaned down, kissed her lips softly. "Please."

"Damn you."

"I'll drive, so no way you'll get another ticket."

"You'll bring me back when I'm ready?"

"Say the word, you'll be right back here."

* * *

The way he kissed alone made giving him another chance worth it. Marcia already knew how good he was in other ways. Would one more time, one more hour, maybe a night, be wrong? This time she took the liberty of looking around, mostly to make sure no one else was there. A whirring noise from behind made Marci jump, and Slick wrapped an arm around her waist. "Just the car coming up." He twisted her to face him. "No one is here but us."

"A girl can't be too sure with you." Grinning, she pulled from his arms and walked to the bank of windows in time to see the sun set beyond the tall buildings. "What a hell of a view." She turned and rested her hip on the sill. "So how does one get an apartment here?"

"Ah-hah, you're looking to get an inside track with the owners of my building."

"Not really, my father could do that."

"You think?"

"We're not on the best terms right now." No way would she tell him the last boyfriend was the reason. Marci had a hefty trust fund bestowed on her by her father and he knew each time she took an extra penny, which he blamed on her ex. Slick didn't need to know that.

He strode to where she rested. "Can I get you anything?" He leaned down and kissed her neck. His mouth was hot, and when his tongue touched her pulse, Marcia's heart skipped a beat. Resting his hands on her thighs, he nudged them apart, and lodged himself between her legs. "Hell's sake, you're hot."

"Me, physically…"

"Your pussy, it's hot against my dick, sweetheart."

"Slick, what do you expect from me?"

"No more than you gave the last time." He kissed her eyelids, the tip of her nose. "I plan to give you more."

"Hmm, is that even possible?"

He moved his hand to the top of her pants. "With you, the possibilities are endless." After loosening the button, he slowly pushed the zipper down. "The first time we were together I didn't get to taste you."

"You didn't? I thought we kissed."

He chuckled in her ear. "No, sweetheart, I mean this." Air puffed from her lips when his fingers slipped into her pussy. "I thought about how tight and good this was every night." He moved his fingers in and out while his thumb rubbed circles around her clit. "But I never got to taste it, feel my lips pressed right here."

"Unnhhh, Slick," she moaned when his fingers left her and he pinched her labia. "Oh G--" His mouth covered hers, smothered her words and any thought she had other than getting out of her pants. His tongue pushed into her mouth, fingers stroked back into her pussy. This man satisfied her from head to toe, and Marcia meant to take all she could get tonight.

Enough to remember when he was gone.

Pulling back, he peered into her eyes. "I don't want to go anywhere." He pulled his fingers from her again, eased them out of her pants. "Did you want to go someplace?"

It was as if he'd read her mind, and that should have shaken her, but it didn't. Marci wanted Slick. "I'm not going anywhere."

"Wonderful." He licked her lips. "Because I want you, here, tonight." He pulled her shirt up and over her head. "Hmm, no bra." He raked his fingers through her thick, brown hair. "Damn, I forgot how beautiful you are." Slick leaned to pull her shoes off before slowly removing her jeans. "I don't want that to happen again."

"Me not wearing a bra, or you taking my shoes off?"

"Smart-ass." He tweaked a hard nipple with his thumb and finger. "I don't ever want to forget how beautiful you are."

"I think I like that."

"What else do you like?"

Marci rubbed his cock with her palm. "This." She moved her hand to his waistband. "Am I going to be the only one naked for the world to see?"

"Hell, no." He eased from between her legs and quickly removed his clothing. Gripping her waist, Slick pulled her up, twisted her to face the window, and pressed her against the cold glass.

"Shit, it's cold!" There were so many lights blazing in the surrounding buildings, could people in some of those rooms or offices see her? Would they watch him fuck her? "Slick?"

"You want to feel heat, sweetheart?"

Warmth enveloped her, made her forget who might be watching.

Glancing at his reflection in the glass, Marcia was sure she saw a glint of red in his eyes, but it vanished quickly. *Must be the lights.* The man behind her, naked and ready to take Marci, was somehow wiggling his way into her heart and her mind. She probably shouldn't do this but no way did she want him to stop.

The only other person who knew about her illicit rendezvous with Slick was her friend, Lori Thornton. They'd talked about both brothers, and Lori warned her to steer clear because there was something strange about them. Marci had chuckled and reminded Lori she was also a little strange lately. Seemed she'd picked up the ability to read minds, well, at least the mind of Slick's oldest brother, Wicked. Maybe Lori was right. The red glint in Slick's eyes, his knowing what she thought, those things weren't normal. But, damn, she wanted to have him again, and hell, that wasn't normal either. Marcia not only wanted him, she needed his arms around her, his cock buried deep inside making her come over and over again.

"I want you to come for me, sweetheart."

He swept her sides with his hands, fondled her ass cheeks. "How'd you know what I thought?" Would he tell her if he could read her mind? His brother had some kind of connection with Lori, who had become frightened enough to stay away from the club. Marci wondered if she should be afraid of Slick and how totally wrapped up in him she was becoming. Yet, here she stood in his apartment, at least she thought it was his, naked, pressed to a window large enough for the world to see what she was doing.

And Marci didn't want to stop.

"I haven't thought about anything else." He kissed her lightly. "I hoped you felt the same way."

Peering at his reflection, afraid to turn and face him, she whispered, "I'm not sure this is right." Her last feeble attempt at stopping what she knew would feel so damn good. "I know I want you, it just doesn't make sense."

"Does it have to make sense, baby, can't you just let it happen?"

His lips were warm against her neck, the glass was warm, the air surrounding her grew warm, and the liquid slipping from her pussy was so very, very warm. "Damn you, take me, make me come for you."

Just tonight, just once more.

"No, Marcia, after tonight, you'll be mine forever." She felt his cock press into the crease of her pussy. "And no one touches what belongs to me."

What the hell!

Chapter Three

Slick hadn't had a woman since the night in her SUV.

He nudged his dick through her moist crease, reveled in the silkiness he found there and wondered if he could stave off coming long enough to satisfy her first. "Shit, you're wet." He planted kisses on the back of her neck. "Would you really care if someone sees me fuck you?"

"I feel like you're reading my mind, and I-I don't..."

"Don't what?" He backed away from her, pulled her far enough from the glass to grasp and pinch her nipples. "Talk to me. Tell me what you don't want."

"Slick, please," she whispered, her breath fogging the window.

"Say it."

"I want it all, and I don't care who sees you fuck me."

"That's my baby. Bend over." He dropped to his knees. "Let me see my pussy." She did as he said, and Slick leaned in, swiped his tongue through her nether lips, sucked and teased her labia. He poked his tongue against her clit, swirling around it, taking every drop of moisture residing there. "You taste better than I could have ever imagined."

"More. I want to feel your tongue inside me."

One hand rested on her ass, the other spread her thighs wider, giving him access to send his tongue as deep as it would go. In, out, he stroked and tasted, took all he could get. Marcia's knees flexed. She widened her stance and pushed her hips higher in the air, letting Slick know she was on the verge of coming.

He stopped licking and teasing long enough to say, "Let it go, sweetheart. I will make you come again." He blew a breath of air against her labia before he moved his tongue back inside her cunt.

"Yes, oooh, yes!"

Slick pulled his tongue back and forth through the warm folds of her pussy before stabbing inside her again. He allowed his tongue to thicken, lengthen just enough to give her more satisfaction.

"Now... unnhhh, now," she moaned while gyrating her big ass, pressing it against his face. "Oh, Lord, I'm coming." He ignored the building swaying, doubted she even felt it as he continued to jab in and out and stealing every drop of cream slipping from her.

Finished tasting her, Slick stood, intending to take her from behind with her breasts pressed against the glass. "I want the world to watch me have my pussy." He placed an arm around her waist, nibbled at her shoulder, and then he bit her.

"Oww, damn you!" she cried as she pushed back into him.

"I'll take the pain away, sweetheart. I'll take all your pain for the rest of your days." He licked the spot, knew tomorrow Marci would be unable to find the wound, and he'd explain it somehow. Right now, Slick needed to taste everything she was. Her cum, her blood, all of it belonged to him. "I'll never let you hurt again."

Like a hellcat, she twisted in his arms, bending her head to capture one of his nipples where she latched on and sucked until drops of pre-cum pulsed from his dick. "Yeah, hell's sake, bite it, Marci. Bite and taste me, sweetheart." Her tongue circled the nub, and her teeth nipped him softly. "Do it, baby. Claim what's already yours." When she bit down, Slick bellowed with delight. "Ahhh, hell, yes!"

Lifting her, he pressed her back against the pane. "Wrap your legs around me, and hold on, sweetheart. I'm going to fuck you until cream pours from your cunt." He thrust his cock to the hilt inside her. Slick pressed his lips to hers, pushed his tongue into her mouth and kissed her long, deep, searching and tasting every corner. Pulling away, he gazed at her face. "Open your eyes. Look at me. See how much I want you."

Marci opened her eyes, and called his name. "Slick, oh shit, Slick." She hiked up and down on his cock, taking it deeper each time. "Don't let me go. Don't stop."

"Never." He continued to slam into her pussy, and her back, covered with sweat, slipped easily up and down the glass. "Damn, I've wanted this tight pussy." His hands were full of her ass as he levered Marci up and down on his dick, and her fingers squeezed and raked his butt cheeks. "Come! Come all over my cock, sweetheart." He felt her cunt clench and release, and Slick knew she was ready to explode again. "Give it to me." He pistoned his cock in her pussy, harder, faster, ready to send a load of semen deep inside her.

"Slick, *unnhh*, I'm... coming..." She leaned into him and bit into his shoulder, drawing blood.

"Yeah!" he cried. The pain unraveled his orgasm, pulled it from his balls through his dick where it met hers head-on. Cum, hers and his, slipped around his cock, and Slick groaned when he felt the warmth of the liquid slide down his thighs. "Damn, baby, you're fucking awesome."

"Lord, Jesus, you're good." The floor shifted, the girders in the building squealed as the tower rolled left then right. "Holy shit, another earthquake!"

Slick tightened his arms around her. "Honey, you have got to stop calling on those heavenly bodies."

She leaned back, peered at him. "Do you really not love Go…"

His mouth covered hers, meant only to quiet her, but he couldn't pull away. His tongue delved inside, and Slick kissed Marci until she struggled to breathe. "Sorry, sweetheart, I got carried away." He loosened her legs, and setting her feet on the floor, he held her until she grew steady. Leaning in, he kissed the tip of her pert nose. "I haven't been with a woman since you." Why Slick felt the need to tell her perplexed the hell out of him.

She looked up at him with eyes stretched wide. "You are kidding?" Staring at his chest, she moved her fingers to his brand. "Why a pentagram -- wait, it's not a tattoo -- shit, it looks like a brand."

Talking about his brand may distract her from his revelation about not having sex. "My brothers and I did it one night fucking around. It's a way to tell us apart. I'm the third triplet, so number three is circled." Sounded plausible, and part of it was true.

"Must have hurt like hell." She peered under her lashes. "You are kidding about not having sex for so long, right?"

Shit. "You make it sound a crime or something."

"It's just, well, you're finer than fine, and could have any woman you wanted." She cocked her head to the side. "How did you release the pressure?"

"Like this." He started to stroke his flaccid prick, grinning at the look on her face when it poked her belly. "When you have the right vision of loveliness in mind, it's a good thing."

"You mean you jerk off thinking about me?"

"Yeah, sweetheart. You." He reached out and cupped her chin. "Your beautiful eyes, your milk chocolate skin, that big ass of yours. Hell, I want to come every time I think about it."

"You're nuts."

"No, I'm…" Slick stopped. *I'm what*? The words were on the tip of his tongue, but he couldn't say them. "I'll show you the shower." Releasing his dick, he grabbed her hand and pulled her in his wake through the master suite, his dressing room, and into the spacious bathroom. "Use anything you need." He turned to leave because if he looked at her Slick was afraid he'd reveal how much he really cared. Would that be so bad, and was it too soon for her? After all, she'd changed the subject when he asked if she was sure she'd gotten over her boyfriend. Marci wasn't like Waverly, Sly's woman. She had no knowledge about the good and evil existing side-by-side in the world.

Marcia had no idea at all a son of Satan had screwed her a second time.

Or that she belonged to him.

Slick damn near hit the ceiling when his brothers laughed and Sly said, "You're in for a raft of shit, man."

"What the fuck? Get out!" He didn't bother to cover himself. They'd seen it all before.

"You're slipping badly if you don't hear or smell us coming."

Sly was right, but damn if he felt like dealing with them right now. "Just go already. I got enough shit to deal with."

Wicked stared at him. "You were going to say it."

Fabricating a pair of cotton slacks, he covered his nudity. "Say what?" Slick walked to the window, picked up Marci's clothes, and deposited them on a nearby chair. He stared out at the gathering stars.

"You know what." When had Wick become such a homebody?

"Hell's sake, don't you have somewhere else you'd rather be?" His eldest brother was right. *I love you* had been on the tip of his tongue, and it scared him shitless.

The stench of sulphur filled the air and their father appeared in a swirling mass of gray smoke. "What has happened to you all?" He waved his hand toward Sly. "Ever since he found someone, you seem to be at each other's throats." Slick turned to see a look of sadness in Lucifer's eyes. "I may not be the angel you would have chosen for a father, but I'm the one you got, and I can tell you first-hand how badly it hurts if you fuck up with someone you should love and hold dear."

He didn't want to cause any more anguish, but he needed the three of them to get the hell out. "This is important to me. Marcia is important to me. Is this a conversation we can have another time?"

"No, it's not." Satan shook his head. "You're brothers. If you can't get along, I will do whatever is necessary to make sure you do."

The bedroom door opened and Marcia, wearing a red robe from his dressing closet, spoke peering back at the floor beneath his bed. "What's with the pentagram on the carpet?" She took two steps into the room, looked up, and came to a dead halt. "What the..."

Wicked spoke first. "I can't seem to keep my little brother out of my home, and I hope like hell the two of you did *not* do the nasty in my bed."

Slick pivoted toward Wick. "You need to cut this shit out."

"Or what? I think it's time you get a job and find a place of your own." Wicked walked into the kitchen followed by Sly, who chuckled.

"Who is this?" Marci glared at him but pointed to his father. "Please tell me there aren't four of you son-of-a-bitches?"

With his brothers so near, their strength coursed through his body, giving him courage. Slick decided on the truth. At this point, it couldn't make matters worse. "Marcia Carter, meet my father, Lucifer."

* * *

Marcia twisted her head slowly and stared with her mouth open. Looking back at Slick she said, "Next you'll tell me it's his face and sexy body on the ceiling in the lobby and he owns the building, which is inhabited by demons from Hell."

The man Slick called father moved to stand in front of her. "I do look sexy in that painting." He smiled and the stars outside the window grew brighter. "Fucking Michelangelo. He was the best at capturing our heavenly beauty." He lifted her hand and kissed the back of it. "My youngest son seems to be enamored with you."

"Okay, this shit is getting weird. I don't know whose apartment this is. All I know is I'm grabbing my clothes and going into the bedroom to dress." She stared at Slick. "When I come out, maybe the twilight zone will be gone." Marci spotted her things on a chair by the window. Picking them up, she walked quickly back into the bedroom, closing the door behind her. She knew she was in deep shit when her body began to tremble uncontrollably. "Twilight zone, my ass. This is the fucking outer limits, and I pray to God they let me leave this place in one piece." The building did another weave and bob, causing her to fall to the bed as she struggled to get her legs in the pants. "Damn, damn, damn!" The building stopped shaking long enough for her to stand and fasten her pants. "Jesus, help me." The building bowed right, and then left. A funnel of white smoke appeared in the center of the room, and a tall, regal woman with blonde hair stepped from the mist toward her. "Oh shit."

"Do not worry. I am a friend."

"Look, lady, the devil just kissed my hand, and I'm standing on a pentagram in someone's bedroom." Marci stepped back. "That worries me." Her calves hit the mattress. "If you come any closer, I'll scream."

"Don't cause my baby boy stress." She smiled at Marci. "I cannot allow that."

Marci searched the woman's blue eyes. Yeah, they matched the blue of the triplets' eyes. "Who the hell are you?"

"I'm Sly's mother, Josette, wife of Satan. Or Lucifer, if you prefer."

"I prefer getting the hell out of here." *Or waking up!*

"I can arrange it."

"I don't want to walk back through there." Marcia felt the heat rise in her cheeks. This woman loved the freaking devil, bore his sons, yet here Marci stood wanting to get away from one, no, all of them. "He might be your husband, but in my book, the good book, he's the goddamn devil."

"I understand." She inched closer, and whispered, "But aren't they beautiful?"

"They have your eyes." Again, her cheeks flushed. Dang, those boys all had one thing in common with daddy. A huge thing. She hoped like hell Slick's mother did not know what she thought.

"Ahh, you noticed." Her laughter tinkled around the room.

"How'd you know… ewww, I don't want to talk to you about Slick's anatomy."

"I'm talking about Lucifer, honey." She gripped Marci's hand. "Are you sure you want to go? Because you can't go back if you leave him now."

"Whoa, hold on. Where are you taking me?"

"Out of here."

"Let me think a minute."

"Do you fear him?"

"Satan, hell yes."

"I'm talking about Slick."

"Josette, right? Can we stick to one person at a time?" She flopped onto the bed and massaged her temples. "Slick doesn't scare me." She sat up scowling. "Has he put some kind of spell on me or something?"

"No, he told his brother he could win you without entering your mind."

"But he could if he wanted to?"

"Yes." Her blue eyes darkened. "The power the four of them hold could destroy this universe."

"Holy Mother of…"

"Shhh! Do not utter holy words, it upsets Satan."

Marci jumped to her feet. "Holy words cause the earthquakes?" She shook her head. "That explains him not wanting me to use them." Marci nibbled on a fingernail while she processed the mess she'd gotten herself in. "And I accused him of not loving God." The floor shifted beneath her feet.

"I'm sorry, we must go."

Slick's mother hugged her, and feeling the air whip around them with frenzy scared the crap out of Marci. It wasn't all that scared her. Before vanishing from the bedroom, Marcia heard something far more horrifying.

A bellow of rage so full of pain, it wrenched her heart and banged it against her rib cage. "No!" She cried out as the ceiling opened and a vortex of air pulled her into the night. "Slickkk!" Marcia cried, tumbling through space with Josette holding her. Fear left her and all she could think about was the agony she'd heard in his cry. "Don't let me go."

Josette answered, "I will not."

But she hadn't meant those words for her.

Marcia uttered them, hoping against hope Slick heard her.

Chapter Four

Slick's bellow of rage broke every piece of glass in his apartment. Doors split in two as his flailing tail scored the wood with deep gouges. His claws shredded everything they touched. Dropping to his knees, he cried, "No, no, no," as he felt her drift away from him. He bent to the floor and banged against the wood beneath him, leaving the imprint of his fist. Feeling his brothers watch him, he lifted his head and stared at them with red eyes. He knew the tears rolling down his face stained his cheeks, and didn't care they saw him in such a weakened condition.

Wicked walked over and dropped down beside him. "It's okay, brother. It is not weakness. I've got you." He hugged Slick to him. "We'll find her."

Soon, Sly was there. "Mother is wrong, Slick, and Wick's right. We'll find her."

"Josette wouldn't have been able to take her if He had not given her such power." Satan leaned through the window frame, stared up into the night sky. "Why have you hurt my son, God?"

Three sets of blue eyes turned toward the twisted metal that had held the glass, expecting the worst. No bolts of lightning, no flames licked through the opening singeing their father. The only change was a crisp breeze blowing through the room, and before they could blink, everything was back as it should be. Lucifer stepped back, allowing glass to fill the window frames.

Slick sucked in a lungful of air. "Look." He pointed toward the moon. A red teardrop slid down and dropped into the night.

Their father's head bowed as if in prayer, and he whispered, "I will never *not* love you."

He turned to his sons. "I cannot follow you."

"I'm not sure what you mean?" Hope blossomed in Slick's chest.

"The red teardrop. It will lead you to her."

Slick's tail disappeared, talons and horns followed suit. Fully clothed, he stood and walked to his father's side. "What have you given up?"

A gaping hole full of flames opened in the floor. "If she wanted to leave, Slick, she will be gone from you forever." Lucifer stepped into the abyss and vanished. The floor slowly moved back into place.

"Why? Why did mother do this?" Slick gazed at his brothers. "And what has father given up for me?"

Sly turned to Wicked, which caused Slick to look at him. Wick rubbed his face before looking at them. "Mother made me a promise." He shrugged. "I thought this was another game like the one she played on Sly and Waverly."

"Shit, I didn't think it was funny. Neither did Wave. She has forgotten it, but damn, mom scared the shit out of her for a long time." Sly's gaze encompassed both brothers. "Sometimes she's not the heavenly creature we think she is."

"He," Slick looked skyward, "is not always sugar and spice, either." A bolt of lightning flashed across the black sky. "Guess we'll leave that alone." Slick was unable to get in his older brother's head. Didn't matter. "I don't need to know what she promised, Wick. I love you, man." He hugged him. "Whatever it is must be important to you, so it's important to me." Thinking about Marcia, he said, "Ready to do this?"

Wicked pierced him with a look, one eyebrow raised. "You showed some power back there." He squeezed Slick's shoulder. "I hadn't realized how much you've grown up."

"I just want my woman."

"Let's go get her."

He bit his bottom lip. "I won't hurt Mom."

"Leave her to me." Wicked vanished into the night. Sly and Slick were fast behind him.

* * *

Marcia opened her eyes and jolted back in the seat. Damn if she wasn't sitting at a table in the club she visited practically every night. The DJ stood behind his equipment spinning jams and adlibbing as usual. She turned to find Slick's mother staring at her with a serene smile, and beside her sat a woman Marci had spotted here often until she hooked up with Slick's brother, Sly.

She smiled and winked. "Hell of a family, isn't it? I'm Waverly. Call me Wave."

"How'd we get here?" Marci knew but she needed to hear it. "And Slick, will he be okay?"

"I whisked you away before you could utter another holy name, and Slick's fine. His father would have it no other way." Sadness settled in Josette's blue eyes. "They have such a small piece of me."

Marci had many questions, but one she needed answered immediately. "Is he evil?"

"Satan?" Josette shrugged. "Only as evil as," she pointed up, "*He* will allow him to be."

"I mean Slick." Josette examined her fingernails, and didn't answer Marci. "So, God has control of -- of your... husband, who happens to be the devil, and Satan has control of his sons?"

"He put the devil here, and then I came along." Blue eyes darkened. "Our God is a jealous deity.

Lucifer and I fell in love, but He never let him go." She looked at Marcia, her lips curved a tiny bit. "Satan will always love me, but I'll always be second best."

"There is a distinct balance between good and evil. Both have their place." Waverly joined the conversation as she leaned closer to Marcia. "If anyone could harm the devil, every angel in Heaven would be on their ass."

"You're kidding?"

She chuckled. "Without Sly, Slick, and Wicked's father, why would we need an angel?"

"Shit." Marci had never thought about it like that. She glanced at Wave. "How do you fit into this?"

Looking at Josette, Sly's woman laughed. "Big bad momma did some research, discovered my tie to Heaven, and she thought I'd be perfect for Sly." Patting the angelic woman's hand, she added, "And damn if she wasn't right. I didn't think I could love anyone that hard or that much."

"It doesn't bother you who Sly is?" Marcia had trouble believing her, especially if Waverly had ties to God.

Josette laughed, a sound so joyful heads turned. People smiled and nodded in their direction. "Honey, don't worry. Good has, and always will, hold the upper hand. All I want is for my sons to find happiness." Her head tilted. "Strangely enough, I want them to know God as Satan does."

"Why did you take me from Slick?"

"I didn't."

"He sounded so hurt and full of pain." Marcia struggled to clear the memory of the sound Slick emitted. "I don't want to leave him."

"You haven't. I just thought we needed a girls' night out. So, ladies, let's have some fun." Josette jumped up and moved to the dance floor.

Marci turned to Waverly. "What the fuck?"

The woman hunched her shoulders. "From experience, I will only tell you this isn't over." She twisted to watch Josette spin around the floor, and then turned back to Marci. "If you ask me, *she* is the goddamn devil, but I like her." She reached for Marci's hand. "Let's dance."

Soon the floor was full of sweaty, gyrating bodies moving to the music. The DJ did his job well tonight. The floor thumped with bass as he ramped up the party sounds. Marci loved dancing; it freed her mind, released her inhibitions, and allowed her to feel alive. Closing her eyes, letting the night sink in, Marcia swayed and moved, giving herself up to the music.

Trying to make sense of it all.

* * *

"What if she wanted to leave me?" Slick stood with his brothers, watching the three women dance around the floor. Patrons not dancing talked, laughed and constantly called for refills. The joy and happiness in the place suffocated Satan's triplets.

Wick's lips tilted at one corner. "Hell's sake, I think I might be named after one of mom's worse traits."

Sly laughed hesitantly. "She is one wicked mother."

"So what do I do?" Slick felt unsure of himself. "Fuck's sake, all this happy juice mom dumped is choking me."

"Don't go all soft now. Shit, you just ripped apart one of daddy's favorite demon penthouses."

"Yeah, and you know who fixed it. Why?" His eyes followed Marci around the floor. The brothers had been forced to meld their minds together so Josette wouldn't know they were there and possibly whisk Marci away again.

Suddenly, Sly huffed in a big breath. "What the hell is Wave doing here?"

Wick threw his head back and laughed. "You don't allow her to come out or something?" Piercing Sly with a look, Wick asked, "Please do not tell me you still don't read her mind?"

"Fuck off, Wicked, she can come and go as she pleases."

Slick chuckled as his brother jammed his hands in his pockets. "I don't invade Marcia's mind, either."

Wicked's blue gaze moved back and forth between his younger brothers. "Are you two stupid?"

"Let it go, we're not like you." Sly watched Wave and used a hand in his pocket to shift his dick. "If anyone even bumps into her, I'll rip their goddamn head off."

Slick punched Sly's shoulder. "You're nasty. Anyway, it's bound to... hold up, did you feel anything?"

Wicked peered around the room. "No."

"Exactly, and after what Sly said, the room should be jumping more than the music." He searched until he spied his mother. "Mom's not reacting, either."

"So what the fuck?" Sly's hands were out and he rubbed his fingers together. "Shit is weird, man."

Slick watched a man bump into Wave, and the music screeched to a halt. "Put your fucking hands back in your pocket if you can't control yourself." He waved a hand and the sounds started again.

"Oh, right, just wait until the son-of-a-bitch walking toward Marci touches her."

"No fucking way is he touching my old lady." This time everything, and everyone, ground to a halt. "Bastard."

Wicked's eyes squinted toward their mother. "She's fucking with us. Look at her eyes."

Josette's blue eyes glittered with mischief, and then she winked at them.

"I've been winked at by her and Father enough to last a lifetime. Wicked, get her ass off the dance floor." Slick fidgeted from foot to foot.

His oldest brother peered at him. "Hell no, you get her."

Slick reminded him of their conversation. "You said to leave her to you."

"Before I realized just how much power she's garnered from somewhere."

"An angel, maybe?" Sly's mind weakened as he attempted to touch Waverly's mental path. "Somebody needs to do something because I'm going for Wave."

Their mother approached them. "Goodness, you boys work well together. She clicked her fingers and the club returned to normal.

Slick felt a surge of energy in his mind before Wick snapped out of his head. He pressed fingers to his temple, and saw Sly do the same thing. What the hell!

Wicked emitted a sinister chuckle. "An easy feat." He clapped his hands together, and then spread them wide. A wave of heat banded around the room, forming a shimmering bubble-like shield. "Break that bitch open."

Josette's eyes darkened. "What did you call me?"

"Mom, please, you know I meant the shield." He grinned. "But if the shoe fits, wear it."

"Why, you…"

"You what? Son-of-a-bitch, motherfucker, spawn of Satan? What, Mom?" He turned to Slick. "Get your woman, little bro." He grabbed his mother's arm.

"Ooh, Lucifer will get you for manhandling me."

"Where do you think I got the extra power, Mommie Dearest?" Wicked grasped her around the waist and vanished.

"Let's cool this shit down and skedaddle." A fresh breeze of air circled the club, disseminating Wick's bubble of heat.

Sly glared at him. "Where did you get such a silly ass word?"

"Go to Hell. I like it."

His brother laughed. "I'm good. Wouldn't want to be there when Josette shows up with Wick." He clapped Slick on the shoulder. "We do work well together."

"I'll see you later?"

"Yeah, bring Marcia for dinner one night."

"Hopefully she wants me."

"Her loss if she doesn't see you for who you are."

"A son of Satan?"

"We're much more than just his sons."

"Thanks, man." Slick strode onto the dance floor, grasped Marcia around her waist from behind, and whispered in her ear, "Come with me, baby."

"Slick!" She twisted in his embrace.

"It's me, sweetheart."

"You let me go."

Her heart pounded against him, and Slick hoped it was because he'd come for her. "Come on." He pulled her in his wake through the crowd and down a dimly lit hallway. "If I'd thought I'd really lost you, I'd have torn this city to pieces."

She came to a standstill. "You are your father's son." Her hands pressed his chest, attempting to shove him away. "Don't. Touch. Me."

"Marcia, I know you've taken in a lot, but I'm not letting you go."

"Why, damn it? Have you put some kind of spell on me?" She cocked her head. "Like you did my boyfriend?"

Okay, she'd figured that one out. "You wanted it."

"No, I didn't. What I wanted was to get rid of his deadbeat, card-playing ass."

"You said you wanted to come more often. I made it happen."

"Even when I was with him, you still desired me?"

"I desire all of you, and you're now aware I'm not a saint." Slick licked his lips, could still taste her there. The shit in his apartment was crazy, but he needed to make Marcia understand. "I've never delved into your mind, and I've not tried to change it even though I could." He snatched her against his body. "Feel me, Marci. I'm hard for you and not some tricked-up, mind-raped thing."

"Jesus, you're -- you're the goddamn devil's son!"

This time the floor did jump, but only a little. His father must be very busy with Josette. "Sweetheart, I'm sure by now you know what causes the earthquakes. Could you lighten up on the blasphemy?"

"I can't live without religion, Slick."

"You can have it. It will be a little different."

"A little!"

Grasping her chin, he asked, "Do you want to leave me? Look me in the eye and tell me you didn't like what we did at my place."

A jerky laugh slipped past her lips. "Is it your apartment, or are you poor and jobless as your brother claims?"

"This is bullshit, Marcia. I'm the son of Lucifer, and I can have anything I wish for in this realm. Answer me."

"Slick, I-I, I don't know, so much has happened."

Slick was suddenly very tired. Using his powers to hold the room with his brothers, dealing with finding his mother and Marcia, it had taken just about everything out of him. At this moment, he wasn't feeling powerful at all. "Marci, I am who I am and, in my opinion, I have the best fucking father in the universe." He set her away from him. "And I have the needs of every other man born, but I won't do this anymore." He turned to walk away but stopped. Telling her she belonged to him, and vice versa, wouldn't matter. She had to say the words. Marcia had to tell him she didn't want to leave him.

"Slick, I'm afraid of the devil."

"You don't think I can protect you?" He hadn't done a good job of it so far. Shit. "Babe, I get it, and it's okay. Think whatever about me, but my father would never harm you unless it's meant to be. He is an angel, and only God can change him." No earthquake shook the floor as he spun on his heels and strode down the hallway.

Wicked blasted into his psyche like molten lava. *After what I've gone through, you better get in her head little brother or I'll fucking rip you a new asshole.*

It's done, man. Pain slashed through Slick's brain, dropping him to his knees.

Do it!

Standing, he twisted around to see tears course down Marci's face. "Marci, I can take the memory of all this away." Why wouldn't she say it? Why in Hell's creation didn't he crawl into her head as Wick suggested and just steal what he wanted?

Sly chimed in. *Because you love her.*

"I love you." This time Slick said it because once he walked away from Marcia Carter the pain would be too unbearable to look back. Yet, he still refused to take any thoughts from her. He pivoted and continued down the hall.

His oldest brother still rattled around in his mind. *You're a pussy.*

"Don't you let me go again." Her voice was a raspy whisper, but to Slick it sounded like a thunderclap as he turned to gaze at her. "I didn't leave you, Slick. I begged you not to let me go." She slowly walked toward him. "I heard your cry. Why didn't you hear mine?"

"Hell's sake, baby, I'm so sorry." Slick met her halfway, lifted Marci into his arms, and before they vanished, he said, "It won't happen again."

Chapter Five

Marcia remained dizzy after they exited the vortex of air. "Where the hell are we now?" She thumped his chest with a fist. "Don't you people ever just jump in a car and drive?"

He grinned before he leaned his head down and nibbled on her earlobe. "Isn't it more fun this way?" Standing her in the soft, warm sand, he added, "It's my private island."

Marci held his hand tight as she peered around. "Uh, you do have a house or something here, right?"

"No." His boyish grin tugged her heartstrings. "Let's camp out, I never got to do it as a kid."

"Can't you build one with magic?" Watching his eyes sparkle with excitement made it damn hard to tell him she wasn't a camping type of girl. Also, she still had questions galore about him, his family. "Slick, I'm not going to Hell to visit your family, let's get that straight right away."

The sparkle in his eyes dimmed. "Marci, no harm would come to you there."

"Look, I've been plucked from *someone's* apartment by your mom, and your dad is... Damn, Slick, your father is *Satan*."

"Honey, he doesn't come above often because his powers aren't so great up here." He kissed her forehead. "And I swear to God, it's my apartment." Sand sprayed into the air and the ground shook as waves crashed the shore. "Damn it."

A spout of water surrounded Marcia waist-high and snatched her from his arms and out to sea. "Slick!"

"Fuck me." He shot into the air and followed. "Sorry, babe." Splashing down beside Marci, he put his arms around her. "Come here." He kissed her hard, his tongue vying with hers. He lifted his head, pierced her with a look of pure lust. "He'll scare the shit out of you, but he won't hurt you."

"What about you? Can they hurt you?"

"I can take care of myself." His lips smashed hers again and one hand tangled in her heavy, wet hair. "Hell's sake, I want you."

He lifted her shirt over her head. "I like your breasts bare, don't ever wear a bra." He bent his head and captured one nipple in his mouth. Slick teased it with his teeth and tongue until she trembled. One hand moved to the zipper of her pants and lowered it. Marci briefly thought about stopping him so they could talk, but she wanted the constricting clothing off, she wanted his hands all over her body. There would be time for talking later. "Just get them off already." Her pants disappeared quickly, and the warm water lapping against her skin made every nerve ending come alive with need. "Take me right here, in the water." She reached for his swollen cock, which was sandwiched between their bodies. "Please."

He grabbed her ass, pulled until her legs straddled his waist. "The wildness in you calls to every part of me." He smothered any words she would have uttered. Slick pushed his tongue deep into her mouth, fought with hers as he touched places only he could find.

The kiss grew tender, searching, and it caused Marci to shove him away to catch her breath. "Lord, you are sweet."

"Damn it, babe."

She twisted to look over her shoulder and saw a huge wall of water heading their way. "Oh, no!"

"I got you." Squeezing her ass cheeks tight, he lifted to hover above the water until the wave passed them and slammed ashore. Settling back into the wet warmth, he murmured in her ear, "I'll always take care of you." He reached between them, gripped his cock, and with one stroke he thrust his length inside her to the hilt. "Mine, Marci." He rested his chin on her head and began to jam in and out her pussy. "Sweetheart, you're mine."

She marveled at the feeling of long, hard, thickness invading her body over and over. She constricted her vagina walls, tried to trap him inside, yet Marci wanted his dick ramming in and out until she came. "Slick, give me everything." She laced her arms around his neck and used them to ride up and down his cock, taking Slick deeper with each shove inside her. "More, harder, all of it." She bent to lick and suck the throbbing vein at the side of his neck. Each pulse of blood coursing through him set her body on fire.

"This is forever, Marcia."

"Yes... yes... yes." A band snapped inside her body, loosened an orgasm that careened from her vagina, and cascaded through her channel. "Slick, come... come now." She threw her head back and cried, "Yours, take it, take all of me." Cum slipped copiously from her, surrounding his cock.

"Fuck, yeah!" he yelled as he bent his head and latched onto her shoulder. His teeth sank in, but before she registered any pain, his tongue swept the wound, took away any ache Marci would have felt. His cock shoved quicker, harder in her pussy as he released a jet stream of warm liquid to mingle with hers. "Hell, yes, sweetheart!"

"Hold me. Hold me tighter." Marci stared wide-eyed at the gray clouds gathering overhead. The air became full of electricity and her hair stood on end. Grasping a handful of his hair, she yelled, "You promised!"

* * *

"Hell's sake." The stench of Marcia's fear permeated his nostrils, angering Slick beyond belief. *Wick, Sly, what the fuck!* Standing Marci in the water, he grabbed her hand. "Don't let go, no matter what." Josette's handiwork, no doubt, and he'd make her pay this time. Water spouted around them forming a funnel, and he knew it would cover them before pulling them away from the beach. The fear in her brown eyes tugged at his heart. "Trust me, baby, please."

Her look became icy, and Slick watched as Marci's shoulders straightened. "I trust you, but I'm gonna kick your momma's ass if she drags me away one more time."

Slick's brothers chuckled in his head before a wave sucked them under.

Blubbering and spitting water, Marci sat up in Satan's living room. "Where the hell is she?" She covered her bare chest with one arm, and used a hand to cover her mound. "I will kick her butt from here to…"

"Uhh, babe, I don't think it was my mom."

This time Marci covered nothing as she stood, hands on her hips, and twisted around the room until her eyes lit on Lucifer. "You son-of-a-bitch." Marci took two steps toward his father before Slick thought to clothe her in a long, red cotton gown. "What is it with you people?"

"Are you sure she's a woman?" Satan grinned. "Because she's got some balls."

"I'm sure." Slick walked up behind Marci and encircled her in his arms.

Marci continued to peer around. "Where's Josette?"

"Acckkk, don't call her, she's apt to show up."

Wicked and Sly appeared, and on their heels, a white swirl of mist evaporated leaving the ghostly form of Josette visible.

"Now what?" Sly asked.

Josette pointed to Satan. "Ask your father."

Slick and his brothers turned to Satan. He kept Marci in his arms, afraid she'd vanish if he let her go.

Wick spoke first. "Pops?"

"I hate when you call me that."

His oldest brother smiled. "You prefer the Devil?"

"I'd prefer you all be someplace else, but this needs to be wrapped up evidently." Satan sighed. "Damn, I miss peace and quiet."

"Peace and quiet in Hell? What a joke." Wicked snapped his fingers and a humongous set of doors at the end of the room swung open to release tormented screams and howls, forcing Marci to cover her ears.

"Wick, stop your shit, man." Slick didn't want her to see the lost souls beyond the outer doors of Hell.

His father glared at him. "Why not, Slick? It's a reality she must come to grips with if she's to remain with you and occasionally visit your home." Horns grew long and pointy on his father's head. Yellow talons spiked from his fingertips as his tail wiggled from beneath his ass on the seat. "I am the keeper of Hell's Gate." He glanced at each of his sons.

Marci spun in his arms. "Slick?"

"Don't worry, honey, Slick won't ever wear the crown of thorns." Wicked picked at his fingernails nonchalantly, "Right, pops?"

Slick watched as his brother hurtled through the air and slammed into the huge Hell-Gate, which had closed.

"Call me that once more, I'll rip your tongue out." Satan's hooves struck the floor and shook the room.

"Tsk, it would only grow back." His mother still hadn't fully materialized.

"Mom, what's with the ghostly look?" Slick didn't like her shimmering in and out of focus.

"Ghastly fits better." Satan sneered. "Guess someone won't be happy with your ass until you come clean."

She bowed her head. "The card player."

Marci ripped from his arms. "My ex? What about him?"

Slick watched her closely. Did she still have feelings for the man? Shit, if she did he'd only kill the bastard.

"Then you'd lose her." Sly leaned against his father's throne, staring at Wick. "Don't worry, Wicked would do it for you. Right, bro?"

Standing and dusting his clothes, Wick said, "Damn right."

"Stay the fuck out of my head, Sly."

Marci looked back and forth from each being in the room. "Someone better tell me what's going on."

His mom finally took shape. "My son wanted you from your first night together. I gave him what he wanted." Josette stared at Slick. "Was I wrong?"

"Mother, where is he?" Slick didn't want to deal with this but he wanted everything to be done with. "It's Marci's choice."

"What if she still wants him?" Wick watched Marci.

"I liked him a lot but I wasn't in love with him. However, he's not a bad person." Slick released a loud breath, and Marcia turned to look at him. "If I did want him, Slick, what would happen?" She pivoted toward Josette. "What did you do to him?"

Slick strode to where Marci stood and wrapped his arms around her. "Honey, it doesn't matter."

"To me it does." Marci extricated herself from his embrace. "Tell me."

He gazed at her, wished he could take her from Hell. He shrugged. "Marci, you belong to me." He touched her chest, right above her heart. "I used no magic on you. I left you with him even though I wanted you." Lifting her chin, he looked into her eyes. "Once you gave yourself to me freely, you became mine."

"Answer my question." She glared at him.

"I'd kill anyone in the world to have and keep you."

"Forgive me, my son." Slick twisted to look at his mother, and the glitter in her eyes should have prepared him for how quickly she yanked Marci's hand. Son-of-a-bitch.

"Goddamn you, Josette, if you take her…"

Her vague form slipped into nothingness, Marci once again in tow.

He pivoted toward his father. "Why didn't you stop her?"

He threw his hands up. "I couldn't." His horns, talons and tail slithered back inside his body.

Slick remembered his father had given up something for him to have Marcia. What? "You still won't tell me what you gave up?"

Satan's lips slanted sardonically. "No."

* * *

"Lady, I've had it with your shit." Marcia's hand connected with a now fully visible face. "You have no right." A breeze lifted the red dress Slick had fabricated for her. Marci turned a full circle trying to get her bearings, see where she was. Back on the beach.

Josette stared. "I have every right to make sure my sons are happy." She stepped toward Marci, took her hand gently this time. "You needed time to think before you said something I or his father could not reverse."

"What do you mean?"

"Marci, my boys are the sons of Satan. They have much of their father in them, though he has yet to allow them to take a life." She let Marcia's hand go. "But I don't know how long before one does."

"Why didn't you let me tell him…"

"Tell him what? You hate him? You could never love someone who would kill another so easily?" The woman turned to gaze over the sea. "I've been there, done that." Twisting back to Marci, she added, "Still, I love their father, and will until the end of days."

Slick's mother was right. Marci had intended to tell him she hated him, never wanted to see him again. How in the world did the woman standing before her live with loving such an evil creature? How had she reared his sons knowing one day they'd become what their father was -- the devil? Who actually didn't seem so bad once she gave it more thought.

"They won't become what he is. Well, at least two of them won't."

"Slick?" She squinted. "And don't read my mind."

"He needs your love."

It was Marci's turn to look over the water, listen to the swell of waves as they washed onto the pristine beach. "I do love him." She took a few steps into the water, let the warmth of it wash over her. "Where is this place? Shouldn't it be dark?"

"It's a figment of Slick's imagination. We always liked the water." She smiled. "As for day or night, it's whatever he wants it to be."

"Damn, it's not real."

"In our minds it is."

"He wanted to camp out." A wistful smile curved her lips.

"He's the one who always wanted to have a happy, normal family." She now stood beside Marci. "After he was first with you, he promised not to intervene between you and your lover."

"Why would he hand me over to another man so easily?"

"Is that what you think, that it was easy for him?"

"I'd have scratched a bitch's eyes out for..." Marci turned to see Slick's mother smiling. "I guess you made your point."

"I needed to be sure you loved him enough to understand sometimes things we do for love aren't always nice." Marci watched her look up. "*He's* the master of heartache, but He also gives us enough love and comfort to sustain us through life's pain."

"Take me back."

Josette turned and walked out into the water, her body shimmering in and out of view. "Don't ever strike me again." She vanished, leaving Marcia alone on Slick's imaginary island.

"Bitch."

Chapter Six

"What the fuck, can't we just act like human beings once in our lives?" Slick plopped into the closest chair.

"You want to be like your mother's people 'cause I can make it happen?" His father stood and paced the floor. "Wick took the boyfriend, but I believe he was prodded." Satan paused and studied his firstborn. "What did Josette promise you?"

He shrugged. "Doesn't matter, Slick's my brother, I'd have killed the man so he wouldn't have to."

"I would have killed him."

"Doubtful since you won't even get in her head."

"I did too." A wide grin curled his lips. "She loves me, man."

"Well, damn, ain't you hot shit, all up in your woman's head?"

"Go to hell, asshole."

"Jackass, where do you think you are?" Wick leaned against the door leading to the bowels of Hell.

"Enough!" His father looked weary. "I'm glad you've finally come together as brothers should, but damn, this chatter is getting on my last nerve."

"I didn't kill him." Wicked smirked. "He's just whiling away some time with a few demon friends."

"You wear the number one." Satan moved to stand in front of Wick. "I've lost a part of the two younger boys to your mother." He licked his thumb and swiped a smudge from the pentagram on Wick's chest. "You're mine."

"Yuck, what the hell, po… man."

"You had ashes on your brand. Send the card player home." Twisting toward Slick and Sly, his eyes grew sad. "You're both too fucking heavenly now to kill anyone, so get your women in line because I'm not going to traipse around the universe saving their asses."

Slick didn't like the way his father's brow furrowed. "I'm not leaving until I know what you had to give up."

The devil sat on his throne with a thud and leaned back, closing his eyes. "He didn't ask me to promise anything. God only reminded me who I answer to." Thunder vibrated overhead, rattling pictures on the walls.

"You gave up something."

"Freedom. But I got something also. I get to share you and Sly with Josette, but Wick will be all mine." Sitting up, Satan smiled. "She doesn't know yet."

Sly peered at his father. "What about the freedom thing?"

"I must live with the angelic bitch for thirteen moons."

"Ouch." Wicked threw his head back and laughed.

Slick's father jumped up, striding to where his eldest son lounged against the door. Allowing one talon to sprout from his finger, he traced the pentagram on Wick's chest, drawing blood. "If you ever harm Josette, I'll kill you."

"You truly love Mother?" His brothers spoke in unison with him, and it made Slick happy to have their minds melded so strongly with his again.

Lucifer's eyes glowed red as he pierced each son with a deadly look. "She's mine, and she's your mother." He headed toward the gates of Hell, flung them open, and then turned. "Sly, go home. And Slick, you got someone waiting for you on your fantasy island." Backing into the flames, he grinned at Wicked. "You, my son, will soon learn the true meaning of the words pussy whipped."

"Yeah, right."

Sly joined Slick with a knowing chuckle. "Can't wait to see that shit."

"Screw you, Sly."

"You've got me confused with the nurse, bro."

The floor rumbled and chairs flipped upside down. "Get the hell out of my house." An icy wind blasted through the room, pushing Slick and his brothers on their way.

* * *

Unsure of where to go, Marci sat in the sand and cursed Josette for leaving her with no way to escape. Sifting through her mind, she turned over each piece of information, digesting everything.

Marcia Carter had fallen in love with a son of Satan.

Josette had survived it, so had Waverly, and she knew she would also. Hell, there were probably stranger things going on in the world than her sorry love life. She had been magically pulled from a demon high-rise to a dance club by her lover's mother; then jerked to the unholy halls of Hell by his father, only to be left to her own devices on an imaginary island. Alone.

It hit her that eventually she'd have to tell her family. At least he wasn't poor. "Shit." Things could only get better.

"Better than you know."

She twisted her head around to see Slick standing behind her. God, he looked beautiful.

"Damn, honey." He scooped her into his arms and lifted her into the air before the giant wave swallowed her. "You've got to get a handle on the blasphemy thing."

"Why doesn't your father consider it blasphemy if I take his name in vain?"

"He considers it an honor to be called upon."

"Je…" Slick's mouth covered hers in a bruising kiss. One which tasted good, lasted long, and satisfied her to the tips of her toes. "Yum," she said when he finally pulled away.

"So you love me, huh?"

"Shut up. Will I ever have another private thought?"

"Not from me." He grinned. "I'll keep the others out if you want."

"Can you?"

"Babe, for you, I'd do anything."

"Take me to your place." She remembered he wanted to camp out but she needed the comfort of a mattress under her ass. They'd fucked in her SUV, against his window for the world to see, and in an imaginary ocean. Marcia looked forward to having him in a soft, warm bed.

When they materialized in the apartment Slick swore was his, she jumped from his arms and worked her way through his home, peeping in every room but the bathroom to make sure they were alone. Decorated in red, his office contained a large oak desk flanked by two big, dark brown chairs. The wood floors shone like glass in the moonlight streaming through the window. She couldn't wait to rummage through his bookshelf, see what he liked to read. A huge flat screen TV took up the wall opposite the shelves. Pulling the door closed, she pivoted toward him. "You don't believe in window coverings much, do you?"

"People only see what I want them to." He pushed his fingers through her hair. "I sure. as hell don't want to hide you from anybody."

"Can you make it day or night here like on your island?"

"No, sweetheart, this realm is His."

"Do I need to check the elevators?"

"We're good, babe." He drew her into his arms. "No one will bother us now."

"I'd love a hot shower."

"Help yourself, and I'll be right behind you."

"Don't leave me here alone."

"I won't." He planted a light kiss on top of her head and swatted her ass as she walked away. "I'll be right in."

True to his word, Slick opened the door before she climbed into the shower. "Want your back washed?"

Marci felt relaxed, playful. "Hmm, I like your idea, and there are a few places on you needing attention." He reached out and tweaked her nipple playfully. She adjusted the water and stepped in. Curling her finger, she beckoned him to follow. "Damn, Slick, are you ever not hard?"

"Yeah, when I can't see or smell you." He tugged until her body bumped into his. "Does it bother you?"

Marci fondled his cock, which lay trapped against her belly. She sucked in a lungful of air when it seemed to grow even bigger. "Only problem I see is how to get this all in my mouth." She ran her palm across the broad head.

"You keep playing with my dick, I'm gonna come in your hand."

Dropping to her knees, Marci swiped at a dot of pre-cum with her tongue. She'd forgotten how delicious he tasted. "I think I'm going to like having you around." Her lips covered the tip and she sucked it rapidly, making him groan.

"Shit, babe." He grasped a handful of hair and shoved another inch in her mouth. "Fucking beautiful." Flexing his knees, he eased in and out of her mouth, allowing her time to adjust to his thickness.

Marci took more with each thrust, until he hit the back of her mouth. After constricting her throat muscles around the cap a few times, she pushed him out. Running her tongue over the full length, she lapped at his balls before coming back to the crown. Cum spurted from the slit and slid over the dark, thick head. Circling the tender ridge with her tongue, she savored the salty taste. "Mmm," she murmured before taking his full cock back in her mouth, and down her throat.

"Marci, damn, babe, suck my dick."

Slick jammed in and out as if he fucked her pussy, and she loved it, loved the control she had over him. "Tell me this is mine," she whispered against the smooth tip.

"All of it."

Swallowing his length once more, she received another spurt of cream, and Marci wondered how long she could minister to his cock before she needed it inside her.

Easing from her mouth, Slick gripped under her arms and lifted her up. "We can finish this later. I want your ass in my bed."

"Having you read my mind, knowing what I want, could be a good thing."

He bent, picked her up in his arms, and headed for his bedroom. When they walked through the dressing room, she heard the sound of birds singing. He kicked the door open, and her breath hitched in her throat. "Slick -- how, oh my!"

His apartment was now one big room and they stood in a tropical rainforest.

* * *

"When..."

"The few seconds it took for me to follow you." He leaned down and kissed her softly. "I still wanted to camp out, but figured since you're not the outdoorsy type I'd bring it indoors."

"God, I love you."

The building moved and he laughed at her eyes squeezing shut, and the long groan she emitted. "You'll get the swing of it, babe."

She thumped his chest. "Is there a bed in here somewhere?"

He dropped her in the center of his bed and climbed between her legs. "Hell's sake, I can't wait to be inside you."

"Hey, nothing will bite me, right?"

"Only me, honey." Slick leaned over and pulled a hard nipple into his mouth. He nipped it with his teeth, and then soothed it with his tongue. Leaving her breasts after having his fill, Slick covered her mouth with his as he guided his dick to the entrance of her pussy. "You still wet?"

"I'm always wet with you."

He thrust his cock in her to the hilt and stopped. "Damn, damn, damn." He pulled out, shoved in again.

"Tight. Hot. I love it." Her arms came around him and fingernails dug into his ass. "Harder, Marci, make me feel you, babe." She gripped him until he began to stroke in and out of her cunt. Repeatedly, Slick drove into her vagina, taking everything she offered.

"Slick, mmm, yes!" she cried, arching her body against his. "Fill me up, babe."

"Oh, yeah, I can do that." He slammed his cock back and forth until his nuts tightened with the need to send semen deep into her pussy. "Come with me." Propping up on one arm, he slipped his hand between their bodies, found her clit and pinched it hard.

"Yes!" Her hips spiked from the bed, jammed against him, sending his dick deeper inside her. Rubbing his finger around her clit and stroking her nether lips while he fucked her made Marci squirm.

"Hell yes, give it to me." Slick moved in, out, and he ground against her, slamming harder each time she constricted her vagina around his penis. His balls ached to release his orgasm, but he'd go all night if it took her that long to come.

Her hands clenched his ass cheeks, and she moaned. "Slick, now, oh, oh… coming…" She angled her hips and gyrated until her cream flowed, the warmth surrounding his length. "Fill me with a part of you."

"Ahh, just what I wanted to hear, babe." He pistoned in, out, jamming every inch inside Marci. "Aww, shit, honey, yeah, *yeah*!" His semen streamed into her pussy, giving her what she'd asked for. "Hell and damnation -- this is *mine*!" he roared. A few more strokes, he gave her everything he had in him. Slick flipped to his back, carrying her with him. "Forever, Marcia."

Her head rested against his chest, and when she lifted it, she used her tongue to trace the number three in his pentagram. "Really, this is all mine?"

"Every hellacious inch of me."

The birds stopped tweeting and the trees vanished in a blanket of heat. Music blared from behind the wall, which now stood between his bedroom and the living room.

"Slick, what…"

"I'm going to stop this shit once and for all." He jumped from the bed and clothed himself before snatching open the door and striding into his living room. "Do you seriously have a death wish or what?"

Peering around, he saw Wave behind the counter pouring champagne. "Sly said he missed you."

"Missed me, my ass."

Wicked appeared in the room followed by an unusually strong stench of sulphur, which could only mean he'd gained more power. "Little bro, we thought you'd like to celebrate."

"I will kill you fuckers."

"No you won't." Sly held a flute of sparking gold liquid.

"It's okay."

He turned to see Marcia smiling at him from the doorway, wearing a knee-length black robe. "Babe, I'm sorry."

"Slick, they're your brothers, I somehow get the feeling keeping you apart is not going to happen often." She brushed the front of the robe. "But we do need to get some of my things here. I can't entertain in robes."

Forgetting his brothers and Wave for the moment, he walked to stand in front of Marci. "You're staying with me?"

"Go-- Hell, yes!"

He picked her up and spun around the room. Standing her back on the floor, Slick snapped his fingers and she was clothed in a pair of fitting jeans and a pink tee shirt.

She glanced down, and then back up. "No pink, babe, too girly girl."

He laughed and replaced the offending shirt with one in red. "That's my woman." And he was glad as hell she understood his strong familial tie to his brothers. He did need to set some ground rules, though. "Could you guys warn me in the future?"

Waverly chuckled. "Good luck." She carried a glass of champagne to Marcia. "Welcome to the family."

She took the glass, swallowed some, and said, "Thanks. Hey, how did you break the news to your family?"

"I didn't have anyone to tell."

"I'm sorry."

"I'm okay with it, and now I have these guys and Josette. So, did he tell you about the brand?"

Hell and damnation, he'd forgotten to come clean about the brand. "Uh…"

"Okay, 'uh' means you didn't tell me everything." Marci waited for him to speak.

"Part of it was true. We do have them so we can be told apart."

"And?"

"Mom had dad do it so she could tell us apart when we were kids."

"Damn, Josette is the devil incarnate." She looked at Waverly. "Could you mistake Sly for either of the other two?"

"Heck no, he's much better looking than they are."

"Excuse me?" Marci walked to the bar and refilled her glass. "You've made a grave mistake 'cause neither of them can hold a candle to Slick."

"You can't really tell until you see them in their natural state." Wave walked over and slapped Sly on the ass. "He has the cutest horns and a really long tail." Shaking her head, she added, "Big. Big all over."

Wick grunted. "I'll show you big."

"Wicked, shut up." She stared at Waverly. "You've seen Sly… you mean, he can look like Satan?"

"Honey, wait until you see that shit, then you'll know just how beautiful they are."

Slick threw his head back and laughed at the look on Marci's face. He sipped his drink as he rifled her thoughts.

They all knew her mind when she turned to them and said, "Out, right now, get the hell out."

When they were gone, she stared at him for a long while. "What?" He grinned.

"You get as big as the devil all over."

"Like father, like son." Slick shed his clothes. He released his horns, quickly followed by his talons and his tail. Stomping his hooves, he let the long, leathery appendage whip through the air and grip her by the waist. "Come here, baby." She didn't flinch from him or his deep, gravelly voice. Slick coiled his tail, drawing her closer. "So?"

"Michelangelo would have adored you." A small rumble echoed through the building and the floor thumped up and down a few times. "I think Lucifer is jealous." She reached over and traced the number three on the still visible brand before she pressed her lips against it. "Damn, you are beautiful." She touched his thick cock. "Whew!"

"Marcia..." His demon's body trembled beneath her touch.

"Now, I need my man back."

"Hell's sake, I love you, woman."

Firstborn (Hellacious 3)

J. Hali Steele

Wicked Sathariel, the eldest son of Satan, has finally met his match, and at the oddest of times, she turns up in his head. Accustomed to having his father and siblings rummage through his mind, he can't handle his woman seeing his hellacious thoughts. And when it becomes clear she's heaven bound -- all hell breaks loose!

Lori Thornton's psychic ability is new, and never one to control her temper or her mouth, she often finds herself in bizarre predicaments. One such event is meeting Satan's firstborn and calling him a pretty boy. When his eyes fill with hellfire and he releases horns, talons, and the long, leathery, forked tail that swings treacherously toward her, Lori knows her life is about to spin deliciously out of control.

Chapter One

Lightning slicing angrily through the bough of a tree that stood silent and graceful for hundreds of years, or water carving away deep, parched earth to form a new river -- these were what Wicked Sathariel's thoughts felt like as they tumbled headlong into Lori Thornton's mind.

Tonight, you will be mine.

She'd called her best friend, Marcia, who had called Waverly, and now they all sat in the club Lori frequented until she first met Wicked Sathariel. That night seeped into her thoughts.

Yeah, baby, remember it. Remember me.

She had entered the club with a few other nurses after a hard day of rapid responses and code blues. Admissions arrived as quickly as discharges rolled out. She'd barely ordered her drink that night when he approached. Lori remembered thinking he was a pretty boy. Suave, debonair, and all fluff.

Not Wicked.

She'd since learned he was anything but. Satan's firstborn was hard, cold, and a deadly motherfucker if she'd ever met one. Lori, never one to bite her tongue, had told him, "Fuck off, pretty boy." Yet the words had never breached her lips. She'd said them in her mind as her body quaked with need the closer he got.

Over six feet of hot and sexy walked up to her, and in her mind, he'd whispered, "Magnificent." The man had the makings of an eight-pack strapped across his abdomen, topped by strong, broad shoulders. Designer slacks, probably made especially for him, rode low on narrow hips, and the soft material caressed muscular thighs with each step in her direction. Damn, he was spectacular looking! Dark hair curled at his neck, and the bluest eyes she had ever seen ate her alive.

Why pick her?

Lori was a big, full-figured girl. She didn't have the type of body that attracted pretty boys.

You're just the type I want, and when I crawl between those thick thighs, you'll come again, and again, and…

"Stop!" She pressed her temples.

"Hey, girl, you okay?" Marcia peered at her strangely.

"He's rattling around in my brain, and God knows, I've tried to stop him." Her head shook from side to side. "I can't."

Waverly watched her closely. "Lori, we've gone over this. If your connection is this strong, there is a reason."

"What? What's the reason, Wave?" Marcia had introduced her to Waverly, some heavenly embodiment who brought light into Sly's life. According to the women, they saved both sons from the clutches of evil, and now neither brother had to bring death to a human. Wicked wasn't so lucky according to Marci and Wave. "You both constantly remind me he belongs to the devil." Shit, they dealt with it, so could she. "Damn, it's hot in here." Loosening two buttons on her top did nothing to help.

Are your nipples hard for me, honey?

"Yes… no… please leave me alone!"

"Whoa, Lori, what the hell?" Marci patted her shoulder. "Girl, I told you, give in to it. You're not getting away."

"I'm afraid."

"You shouldn't be. Look at us. We're safe." Waverly smiled. "They're not as bad as you think." She winked at Marcia. "There are some really awesome benefits." The two of them laughed. "Anyway, he can't harm you, Lori. It's not allowed."

A sigh puffed through her lips as she put her elbow on the table and rested her chin in her palm. "I'm not as afraid of him as…"

Both women cut her off. "Then what's the problem?"

"I'm more afraid of me."

"Uh, can you explain that?" Marcia's head tilted.

"I -- you see, well… Damn it." She was at a loss for words. *Kinky* jumped in her mind right beside *ménage* and all the crazy things she wanted to try with him. Who better than Satan's son, right? After all, he couldn't call her…

Oh, you are nasty, and I like it.

The chuckle he emitted rolled around and around in her head. It was nasty, and not something she wanted to divulge to the two women staring at her across the table.

Tell them you want me to smack that ass. Tell them you want to feel my devilish tongue in your pussy.

You know what? You tell them. She grinned, thinking herself safe sitting here with friends who had a tie to two of momma's boys.

The stench of sulfur burned her nose and made her eyes water. She rubbed at them with a napkin, and when she looked up, there he was.

Pulling out the chair next to her, he sat down and stretched his long legs under the table where muscled thighs touched Lori's. "Always good to see my brothers' women." His mischievous grin only improved his sex appeal.

Marcia waved him off. "Don't start any shit, Wicked, I'll call Slick."

Wave nodded. "And Sly."

"I'm wounded you think so little of me." He turned his vibrant blue eyes on Lori. "Surely, you think better of me, lover?"

"I'm not your lover." But, oh God, she wanted to be.

The room shook, rattling the glasses on the table. "You will be."

Her cheeks grew warm, and she damn near whimpered when he flashed his charming smile in her direction.

"And I'll do almost everything you want." His hand touched her thigh beneath the table. "I'm sure you know not to use his name in the presence of any of us. Pops likes to be number one."

"Go to hell." Sweat dripped down Lori's back.

"With you, any time." He eased his hand between her legs. *You're wet.*

The room and everyone in it stilled. Slick appeared behind Marci, and Sly plopped into the seat beside Wave. "I don't know about Slick, but I'll be damned if you're going to terrorize my woman."

"Slick, little brother, help me out here?"

"Hell no, Wick, Marci's not comfortable with the way you've accosted her friend."

"Accosted!"

Lori examined the fruity concoction in her glass, watching as condensation slipped down the side and formed a puddle on the table. It made her think of how a pearly drop might look easing over the crown of Wicked's cock.

Look at me, damn it.

Her head snapped up.

Should I tell them about all your kinky fetishes, honey?

Wicked, please, don't.

One night.

Then you'll leave me alone?

He looked from one person to the other at the table before he spoke aloud. "After tonight, if Lori doesn't want to be with me, I'll leave her alone. Forever."

The others at the table zeroed in on her and Marcia asked, "Lori, you okay with this?"

Unable to form words, she nodded. Wicked moved quietly in her psyche, mentally caressing her nipples. He kissed her neck and sucked her pulse until she couldn't breathe. When she felt an imaginary finger slip into her vagina, she rocked forward on the chair. *Please, not here.*

"Come with me," he whispered in her ear. This time his tongue really lapped beneath her ear and sent shivers down her spine.

"Anywhere." Why had she said that? Jesus, Lori knew who… what the being beside her was. Anywhere could be Hell as far as she knew. At this moment, she didn't care. Without recognizing it until now, she wanted to go with him, stay with him. She'd fought it long enough.

"Heaven, honey. I'm going to take you to Heaven tonight."

The floor swayed back and forth, causing patrons to squeal in fear and shout "earthquake." Wicked threw his head back and laughed. "A metaphor, nothing more, Father."

Lori was afraid because in Wicked's arms she would feel like she had died and gone to Heaven. She feared more than anything, one night might not be enough.

The floor bucked beneath the table, and it was the last thing she remembered before he magically plucked her from the club.

* * *

Wicked remained a little annoyed about what she'd said about him on the beach the day Slick reacquainted himself with Marcia Carter. He lounged against his bar, keeping his hands in his pockets. "So I'm a freaking nutjob?"

He listened to the turmoil in Lori's mind as she peered around his apartment, taking in the dark, masculine furniture, his guitar leaning against the amp by the tall mahogany stool he sat on when he played. *Unbelievable.* "You play guitar?" She glanced at the wall between the loft's two elevators. Brushing her fingers lightly over the strings, she asked, "Who painted the picture?" Lori caressed the neck of the instrument, sending a flare of passion to his crotch as he imagined her fingers squeezing his cock.

The Old Guitarist was his favorite painting, and the reason he played. Wicked found it soothing to coerce sounds from it no one heard but him. He liked having total control over something in his life. "Unbelievable that I enjoy music?" He glanced at the painting. "It is a Picasso." He shrugged. "Over the millennia I have gained some culture, if only by osmosis, honey."

"That's not what I meant."

He strode to stand in front of her. "Tell me, sweet Lori, what did you mean?"

"It's just…" Breath hitched noisily in her throat. "I didn't think, oh hell, you know what I meant."

"Tell me, I want to hear you say it."

"I didn't think the son of Lucifer would play an instrument, enjoy music and art, or -- or read a book." She straightened her shoulders. "In fact, I didn't think you'd be normal at all."

"I am much more than the evil creature you believe me to be."

Wicked hadn't intended to kiss her so soon. He wanted Lori to get used to him. Eyes that rivaled his in their blueness stared at him. She ran a hand nervously through her neck-length blonde hair and her full lips quivered. The smell of her fear made him anxious, unsure. How could he make her understand he'd never, ever hurt her?

"I'm going to kiss you."

When she didn't step back, he leaned down and pressed his lips softly to hers. His hands were now clenched at his sides as he vowed not to touch any other part of her body. Wick knew her wide hips would be soft, her plump breasts would more than fill his palms, and her nipples, taut beneath her shirt, would be so damn sweet. Easing his tongue past her lips, he tasted her for the first time. His senses reeled at the exotic flavor of who she was. Her thoughts, her needs, tumbled headlong into his mind and blinded him with the light of goodness from her soul.

Snatching back, he gazed at her long and hard. "Hell's sake, I didn't expect you to be so fucking devout." Especially knowing what she desired of him. No matter, he would take her tonight, make her his. He ran the tip of a finger around a bud. "Are they hard for me, Lori?"

"Wicked… I… please, don't…"

"I will do nothing you have not dreamed of."

"I didn't realize you invaded my dreams."

"I watched them." He smiled. "I wanted your sleep to be peaceful."

"You can do that?"

"I can do anything I want. I've been through your mind a hundred times since that first night." Shoving hands back in his pockets so he wasn't tempted to touch her again, he tilted his head. "You've been in mine also." He still couldn't fathom how that had happened. Probably his mother's doing. "Have you seen anything terrible enough to condemn me for?" He felt her feeble attempt at reading him, but he'd closed that pathway for now, aware another would only spring up. *Damn Josette.*

"No, but, unlike you, I haven't seen everything. I know it's there. I feel it." She averted her eyes. "You are the devil."

"I am his son."

"Like father, like son."

He moved to stare out the window of his loft. Lights shone brightly from the many high-rises surrounding his building. Looking up, he saw a myriad of stars, and one shot toward Earth in a solitary path. He remembered when he was a boy, Josette told him shooting stars were angels falling to Earth. Wicked never believed it. They were pieces of dying planets or stars, nothing more.

"Tell me what you feel right now."

"I can't."

He turned to face her and rested his hips on the sill. "Yes, you can."

"I want… damn it, Wicked, I want you."

He grunted. "I know what you want. Tell me something else. Something I don't know."

"You know everything there is to know."

"I don't know why it took you so long to come to me." He should have had her in his bed long ago.

"What do you mean?"

"You've known since the first night we would be together."

She stuttered, "I-I guess I did."

"I scare you that much?"

"Yes."

He walked to her. "Yet you envision me between your thighs." He ran a finger over her lips and sighed. "I don't want you afraid, and I won't take you that way." His body shimmered in and out of view. "You will stay here."

"Don't leave me!"

"You can't stand to be with me, but you don't want to be without me."

"Wicked, I need time."

"You've had enough, but I'll give you a little more." He vanished, heading below to visit with his father.

Relax, honey, you got what you wanted. For now.

* * *

"This is unexpected."

"My coming home? Why?"

Lucifer stood and paced the length of his grand living room. "Is this your home?"

"I don't need anyone else fucking with me right now."

His father strode back, fell heavily onto his throne, and laughed, the sound shaking the walls. "Remember me saying you would soon learn the true meaning of the words pussy whipped?"

"Shit, I haven't smelled the real thing yet."

"Hell can't help you when you do."

"Damn it, she's so afraid of me, the fear rolls from her in waves."

"Wicked, you are the firstborn son of someone who people believe to be the most evil creature in the world. What did you expect?"

He rested his head back, closed his eyes, and ran a hand through his hair. "Hell if I know. Why couldn't I simply fall for a demon?"

"Because you are also my son." He sat up at the sound of Josette's voice. She entered the room wearing a white gown that billowed around her.

"Only you would wear white in Hell, mother."

"Haven't you heard? White can be worn all year round now." She flounced on a large pillow at Satan's feet, and he idly played with a ringlet of her golden hair.

"What the hell does that mean?"

She waved her hand. "I don't know. Some fashion cretin deigned it so."

"For hell's sake, I meant... shit, never mind."

She grinned. "Why such unhappiness? You have finally captured what you wanted."

"I didn't want a woman so afraid of me she can barely stand the sight of me."

"That's not true."

He squinted at Josette. "How would you know?" He'd get to the bottom of her involvement in his affair. If she had not learned her lesson after Slick and Marcia, Wicked would teach her.

"Wicked, you have been warned once." The pain inflicted when Satan traced Wicked's pentagram with a talon and drew blood flashed acutely in his mind. "There will not be another warning."

"Damn it, I got it."

His mother laid her head against his father's thigh. "I have lost you."

"You thought to have all three of us tied to your apron strings?"

"That's an ugly picture, Wick."

"Yeah, you in an apron. How unlikely is that to ever happen?"

"You helped me with Slick and I gave you the woman you wanted."

He leaned forward. "What did you give her?" Satan stood and headed for the gates of Hell. Lucifer's grip on him and his mind slipped, and Wicked yelled, "Don't you dare walk through those doors." Wick followed him, stopping just short of bumping into the devil's back. "You did this?"

"Watch your tone. Why do I have to keep reminding you where the fuck you are?"

"For crying out loud. *You* did it. Why, why did you let her see into my mind?" Sometimes tenderness and love dripped from the fingertips of his father, especially when he dealt with his sons. This was one of those times. He touched Wick's cheek with his hand and love poured into him, but the most horrific thing he could imagine quickly followed. The vision overwhelmed Wicked, took him to his knees. "Hell, no… *no!*" His pain expanded, entered every part of his body, and instantly his brothers were at his side.

Sly spoke first. "Easy, man, easy, we're here."

Slick helped him to his feet. "I'm sorry, Wick, so sorry."

They had witnessed the vision also. He stood and glared at his father. "It won't happen. I won't let it."

Satan opened the gates of Hell and walked inside the door. Pivoting, he gazed at Wicked with red tears staining his cheeks. "It will happen."

"Fuck you."

"Wicked!" Josette stood behind him and put her arms around his waist. "He's your father."

Glaring at the doors as they slowly shut, he cried, "He's the goddamn devil, nothing more."

Walls trembled throughout the bowels of Hell, the gates flew back open, and Satan in all his hellacious glory tramped back into the room. Horns glistened, talons appeared longer than usual, and the long, leathery tail whipped high and low scoring the walls with gouges. "You didn't think being mine meant sweetness and light, did you, Wicked?" Satan snatched Wicked from Josette's grip and the talons tore into his flesh. "Did you?"

Wick lost all control. His horns sprouted, followed quickly by talons as pointy and deadly as Lucifer's. A thick, spiked tail waved around the room, sending his brothers and Josette scurrying into the far corner. Fire flicked from his mouth when he spoke. "Release me. I'll show you evil."

Satan laughed, an eerie sound, which gave Wicked pause after he was dropped and his hooves hit the floor. "I made the right choice when I chose you."

"I could have told you that, Pops." Sarcasm laced every word.

"What do you think you're going to do?"

"I'm not going to let you hurt her."

His father chuckled. "I'm not going to hurt her."

Wick breathed a sigh of relief.

"Don't you ever come against me again. And in *my* house?" Satan opened his mouth and a blast furnace of flames licked at Wicked, causing him to back up. "You are much stronger than your brothers, but I can still burn your ass behind the gates of Hell forever." He wrapped his tail around Wicked and flung him to the floor. "Do. You. Understand?"

Wicked refused to give an inch until his brothers drew near and he feared for their safety. "Stop, I'm okay."

Stepping back through the heavy, impenetrable doors, his father smiled. "Wicked, you are firstborn, you are mine, and *you* will kill her, not I." Sadness rested in his eyes as he glared at him. "This is what it's like to reign in Hell, my son. Get used to it." He looked up. "She belongs to Heaven."

Overhead, thunder sent bolts of lightning to pound Earth and shake it on its axis. The doors slammed shut, shielding every dead creature behind it from the wail of anguish that ripped through Wicked's body and emanated from his mouth. "Nooo, God, no!" He came to his knees, tail thrashing and destroying everything in its path.

His brothers pulled Josette beneath them to shield her as stone and glass crashed all around them. His human body emerged, curled into a fetal position, and he watched as his red tears flowed into the crevices of stone beneath him, staining them forever.

Josette crawled to where he lay, pulled him into her lap, and held him. "I know you won't believe me, but he loves you, Wicked. He will take away your pain."

He glared at her. "Your God can't help me now."

"I'm talking about your father."

"Who will take Lori's pain away, Mother? Who?"

Chapter Two

There was nowhere for her to go that Wicked wouldn't find her. Hell, Lori wasn't so sure any more that she wanted to get away from him. She decided to take a shower, then crawl in his bed, and wait. Water cascaded over her back, easing the tension from her muscles. She thought about her friends, Marcia and Waverly. Both were with sons of Satan, had been for a while, and neither seemed to suffer. In fact, the women glowed every time she saw them. Love and happiness surrounded them along with a serene acceptance of their positions. She'd have to reach that point.

Because Lori knew, without a doubt, she belonged to Wicked Sathariel.

After drying herself, she grabbed a long black robe from the dressing room just outside the bathroom and wrapped the silky material around her body. Moving through his bedroom to the door, she made note of the red pentagram on the carpet beneath her feet. Even in this private space, he surrounded himself with signs of his parentage. Closing the door behind her, she went to look out the window.

The view left her speechless. Glass made up the whole wall, and the night was so clear, she could see lights in buildings and homes for miles and miles. She nibbled a fingernail and thought of reasons she couldn't do this. None trumped the reason she *would* do this -- Lori wanted Wicked badly. Even now she tasted him on her lips as she swiped her tongue over them.

Thunder boomed overhead, and a flash of lightning caused her to step back from the window. "Jesus." Another bolt shot straight toward the building, and she shielded her eyes as glass shattered and showered the room with glittering shards. One piece lodged in her shoulder as the back of her knees bumped the sofa, but she barely felt it as pain slammed into her stomach, dropping her to her knees. "Wicked!" Briefly, she felt him in her mind, and then he was gone. Silence. For the first time in months, she didn't sense him or hear him in her head. "What the…" Heat pulsed to her right, and she scooted left until she was practically beneath the large stool flanked by the guitar amplifier. The floor opened and Wicked levitated through the burning hole, followed by his brothers.

"Aww shit, baby, you weren't supposed to feel that." He strode to where she hid, and stooped down. He lifted and carried Lori to the sofa. His eyes flared red for an instant. "It will never happen again."

Slick appeared worried. "We can stay, you might want to talk."

Wick combed fingers through her hair, and as he kneeled to pull the robe around her, he noticed the shard of glass. "Damn, damn, *damn*, baby, I'm sorry." His blue eyes were piercing, appearing almost mirror like. "Look at me."

"It's not your fault, but what the hell happened?"

"Shh, I'm going to remove it, and it won't hurt, I promise." Leaning over, he pressed his lips to hers. His tongue slipped in, and filled her mouth. It was sweet, hot, and everywhere. He touched and tasted every spot he could reach, and she allowed it, giving him just as much back. Her shoulder tingled and felt warm, nothing more. When he withdrew, she licked his lips, not wanting him to stop. "Wicked?" Lori gazed at him, wondering why she couldn't read him anymore. "Why have you closed yourself off from me?"

"What do you mean?" He held the bloodied piece of glass up before he tossed it toward the mangled wall. Metal scraped against metal, reshaping itself, and shimmering like rain, the pieces gathered from the floor, the sofa, everywhere, and it melded back into the frame forming windows. The bloodied piece fit in last and it glowed red in the light. "I like that you are strong and able to stand pain."

She ignored his last comment. "I can't reach into your mind anymore."

He twisted toward his brothers and sat on the floor. "I'm good."

Sly leaned against the stool, hands in his pockets. "You sure?"

"If I wasn't, you'd know."

"Call if you need anything."

"I got what I need right here."

Lori listened to their conversation, and again, she wondered what had transpired during his absence. One thing she was sure of -- the pain she felt was his. In the blink of an eye, his brothers were gone, and the room was full of... of silence. Not even their breathing made noise.

Standing, he lifted her shoulders and sat on the sofa, bringing her back onto his lap. "Don't be afraid of me."

"Wicked, I know you won't hurt me."

"Then why do I smell fear?"

"It's my fear. Fear of what will happen if I become lost in you."

Bending over, he licked and soothed the spot where the glass had been. "I'll find you no matter where you go." He drew her up until her butt rested in his lap.

"Wow, it doesn't hurt." Resigning herself to the fact she belonged to him, she grinned. "Well, if I'm with you, it's not very likely they'll be saving me a seat up there."

"Even in Heaven, I'd find you."

* * *

She belongs to Heaven... The words played repeatedly in his mind, and each time they wove through, the anguish tore at him again. He was glad Lori didn't feel it. He should have done a better job at protecting her from his pain; *any* pain. None of it mattered right now, Lori was in his lap, and she seemed to accept the fact she belonged to him, and always would.

Wicked stripped the robe from her shoulders and with his arm cradling her, he leaned down, drew a taut nipple into his mouth, and nipped it hard.

"Oww, unnhhh, yes!"

He ran his tongue around the bud, sucked and lapped it. Letting go, Wicked moved to the other side. This time he bit harder and was gratified when she lifted her big ass, arching her body and sending the nipple deeper into his mouth. "Feels so good."

"You like it."

"More," she whimpered.

He pushed his hand between her legs and worked two fingers back and forth in her crease to wet them. "You're nice and wet." After teasing her clit, he pinched it, and Lori rewarded him by twisting his nipple hard through his shirt. "Damn, babe, our clothes have to go." With a thought, they were gone. His dick throbbed at the crevice of her ass cheeks, and drops of cum slipped from the engorged head. "Get up." No sooner had her feet touched the floor, he lifted her to the back of the sofa, and rested in front of her on his knees. "Open your legs." He gripped her around the waist with both hands and bent his head between her thighs. His tongue flicked her labia, and then swept through the crease until no cream remained. "Give me a little."

"Lick it, bite me." His teeth nipped her pussy lips and he bit her inner thighs until she swiveled on the sofa back. "Yes, Wick, yes!"

A tiny rivulet of liquid slipped from her. "That's my baby." He tongued her cunt until she squirmed and her hips bucked up and down.

Wanting something more, Wick stood on the seat between her legs. "Suck my cock." He held the back of her head and inched the cap through her lips while one hand gripped her shoulder so she wouldn't lose her balance. Jamming in and out of her hot mouth pulled him to the edge, but he wasn't going to come yet. "Take it all, Lori."

He sent more of his length down her throat until her tongue wrapped and laved his thickness. She controlled how much cock he sent into her mouth and, damn, she took a lot. "Shit, babe, your mouth is wicked good." Her fingernails dug into his ass, pulled him back and forth as she twisted her head. Lori swallowed so much of him, Wicked marveled at the fact she didn't choke. "Swallow it, swallow every inch." In, out he sent his shaft through her lips into her mouth as if it were a pussy.

When she pulled back, she looked up, her blue eyes dark with lust. "How much can you stand?"

Wicked had been in her mind enough to know what she was asking. "Hard, suck it hard, taste it, taste me." When he felt her teeth on the ridge circling the head of his dick, he cried out, "Do it, let me feel it."

When she bit down, he sent cum splashing down her throat. "Fuck, fuck, *fuck!*" He stroked in her mouth until she had every drop of semen.

"Mmm, I like that." She smiled up at him, her lips swollen and sexy.

"Oh, lover, I'm not done with you." Climbing from the sofa, he walked around and grasped her around the waist, pulling her down. "Lean over the back."

"Can you…"

He held a hank of blonde hair and pulled her head back. "Feel this, baby." He thrust inside her cunt with one long, hard, stroke. He went so far, his nuts banged against her. He swatted her big ass each time he jammed his cock in her pussy. "It'll always be hard as hell for you, Lori."

"Yes… yes… yes," she murmured each time he stroked in. "More, I'm there, Wick, harder."

He feathered fingers over the spot his hand spanked as he pounded inside her. Twisting her head sideways, he gazed at her. "You are so damn hot." Leaning down, he bit her shoulder until he drew blood.

"Oh, oh, oooh!" she cried. "I'm coming… yes, *yes.*" Her body slumped forward as cream surged from her.

"Ahh, shit, Lori…" His orgasm started in the pit of his stomach. Wicked closed his eyes, felt the semen travel from his balls to fill Lori's sweet, sweet, pussy. "Take it, take it all, babe." He ejaculated another rope of cum. This time Wicked buried it inside Lori as he fell over her back. He remained draped over her, licking her neck, running his tongue across her shoulders.

She chuckled.

"What's funny?"

"Wicked good?"

"You liked that, huh?"

"I think I'm going to like everything you do to me."

"Good because… what the fuck?"

"Oh shit, sorry, man."

"Sly, turn your fucking head."

"Damn, man, you were up in that."

"Slick…"

A shower of sparks gathered in the air and zoomed across the room covering the front of each brother's slacks.

"Son-of-a-bitch. Damn, Wick, that wasn't necessary." Slick brushed frantically at the fire on his pants.

"I dare either of you to say another word."

"Okay, cool it with the fire on my cock." Water poured from the ceiling over Sly and Slick.

"What are you doing?" Wick had fabricated another long robe for Lori, this one in red, and he stepped from behind the couch wearing a black pair of cotton drawstring pants.

"Hell's sake, did you want me to let my prick burn off?" Sly stood soaking wet in the middle of the floor. With the wave of his arm, the water was gone and both he and Slick were dry. "We came up to…"

The doorbell stopped him. "I can smell Wave and Marci, and someone better start talking."

Slick chimed in. "Sly was trying to tell you we came up with a way to fix your problem."

Marci and Wave walked in and sat on the sofa. Marci patted a spot beside her and told Lori, "May as well sit down, this is where they go all mental on us so we don't know what they're talking about. You'll get used to it."

Wave snorted. "She can read her man's mind."

Lori plopped on the sofa. "Not anymore."

"Shoot, that's not good, we were counting on you telling us."

"Wave, hell and damnation, shut the fuck up."

Sly strode to stand in front of Wick, "Don't talk to her like that. We came up here to help you."

"Someone, please, clue me in." Lori looked back and forth from Wicked to Sly. "I seem to be the only one in the dark."

She doesn't know.

Shit, Wick, you fucked her and didn't tell her?

I'd like to see you tell Wave you were going to kill her.

Uh, that shit happened, remember?

"What the hell?" Wick heard concern in Lori's voice.

Marci looked at Lori. "Told you they'd go all mental. Sly and Slick were at it downstairs, then they said to follow them up here."

"Shit, I can't think with all the chatter. Sorry, babe, this won't take long." Wicked snapped his fingers and the three women vanished.

"Where the fuck are they, Wick." Slick glared at him.

He laughed. "They're on your island, so stop worrying, now, tell me what the hell this is about."

"We have to use our strongest shields so Pops doesn't hear us." Sly sat on the stool and picked up the guitar. "She belongs to Heaven." One finger strummed the strings until Wicked slapped him on the head. "Hey, that hurt!"

"Do you know what that's worth? And I just tuned it." Wicked paced behind him. "Talk."

"Shit, you never play it and you can buy another one."

"It wouldn't be the same."

"Then I'll buy you one."

"Hell and damnation, Sly, give me a break."

"Whatever. She belongs to Heaven…"

"What he's trying to say is if you married Lori all churchified-like, she'd be tied to you in the eyes of you know who." Slick looked skyward. "That way she'd be part of our family, and a sinner."

"Yeah, if she's your wife, then she's bad by association and can't go to Heaven." Sly moved to the window and sat on the sill. "You're not going to get out of killing her, so at least after the deed is done, she can go to Hell and be with you."

Slick still had a penchant to be the good brother. He smiled. "It was my idea, and I think it's a damn good one."

Married! Wick walked over to stand by Sly at the window, and Slick joined them. He watched silently as a shooting star appeared in the dusky sky and seemed to collide with the sun cresting the horizon. "Remember Mom telling us the story about shooting stars being fallen angels?"

Sly peered at him. "You know that's not true, right?" Light blazed around Wicked's body before he disappeared. "Where the hell are you going?"

"To catch a falling star."

* * *

"Where are we?" Lori balanced herself on wobbly legs as she watched water rush over the sand. "I know one thing; everyone needs to stop jerking my ass through the atmosphere."

Marcia laughed and shook her head. "Slick thinks his brothers don't know about his private island."

She grunted. "I get the feeling Wicked knows everything."

"Well, he does have the closest tie with his father."

"What does he look like?"

"Lucifer?" Waverly chuckled. "He looks damn near like they do."

"Damn near?" Lori peered at Wave. "What's different?" Okay, here's where they tell her he has horns and spews fire at those unfortunate enough to find themselves in Hell.

"Most times, nothing."

"Huh?"

Marcia said, "Sit down." She and Wave kicked their shoes off and once they were all sitting wiggling their toes in the warm sand, she started. "Lori, Satan looks like a man. Hell, when I first saw him, I thought there were four of the son of a guns."

"You mean there are no horns and hooves?"

Waverly giggled. "Horns, talons and hooves, just as all the books describe."

"So what aren't you telling me?"

"They *all* have them."

"Good Lord."

A ten-foot wave rushed to shore and washed over them, damn near dragging them into the ocean. "Lori, damn it, there's no one to save us here," Waverly yelled, crab walking backward.

"Meaning what?" She wrung the hem of the robe out and used it to dry her face.

"You have to stop calling on Him," she peered upward, "in any form. The devil doesn't like that people call on you know who, it makes him jealous and he causes earthquakes, storms, and shit."

"You're kidding, right? He gets jealous?"

Marcia pulled Lori's hem out of her hand and used it to dry her face. "I wouldn't test it again if I were you."

"Hey, use your shirt."

"Well, your robe has more material."

"Oh, so just lift it up and show my big ass to the world, why don't you."

"Lori, this island is a figment of Slick's imagination. There's no one else here. It's a place he created because he wanted to go camping as a kid."

"Oh, for the love of G--"

Both women yelled, "Shut up!"

"Damn it, what do we do if no one comes to get us?"

Waverly laughed so hard she doubled over. "Another thing you'll soon find out. If Wicked's anything like my Sly, they are possessive as hell, and you're not going to spend any nights alone or away from him."

Marci nodded. "She's right."

"I don't want to." Lori examined her nails. One night was all she promised, but even as she did, she knew, hoped and prayed, there would be more. Should she tell them all the things Wicked had discovered in her mind? Things she'd kept hidden until she met him?

He'd delved into the dark corners and found all the naughty ideas she had kept tucked away, thinking she'd never find anyone who would understand. She smiled, remembering him say "wicked good." How fitting a phrase.

Oh, the things he could do with... "They really have horns and shit?"

Marci walked to the water's edge and stuck her toes in. Lori and Waverly followed. "I'm cooling my libido off." She glanced sideways. "Girl, when you see him like that, you'll never, ever forget it."

Wave nodded. "Magnificent. Sometimes I wonder what it'd be like to have sex while..."

"Eww, eww." Marci covered her ears. "Too much information."

"But it's so thick and big."

Lori stared at Wave. "You mean their penises?"

"Hell's sake, yes."

"When they have horns and talons?" A vision of Wicked's tail wrapped around her, holding her immobile, and his forked tongue flicking out caressing her in private places jumped into her mind. His thick cock... *Sheesh*!

"Yes."

Marci started to laugh. "Wave saw Lucifer's."

"No?"

"What does it look like?"

"Not quite as big as Sly's but..."

The island tilted and shook under their feet, sending water cascading toward them again. Running inland to escape the giant wave, they banged into Sly and Slick who popped out of nowhere.

"What the hell, Wave, I heard that."

"It's the tru-" Sly slammed his mouth over hers. When the kiss deepened, Marcia cleared her throat. "Sorry." Waverly sucked in a breath of air. "Their father is sensitive about size."

A fissure of white light split the air and Wicked appeared. He strode toward Lori and dropped down on one knee, holding out an odd-looking ring. "Lori Thornton, will you marry me?"

"Oh, Jesus!" The sky opened up and hail and rain slammed the beach, spraying sand in every direction.

"Is that a yes or a no?"

"Yes!"

He slipped the ring on her finger, picked her up and spun in a circle while rain slashed them from every side, soaking their clothes. He grinned mischievously. "My dick's the biggest." Again, the vision popped into her head of his swollen cock. Lori knew Wicked projected the picture in her mind and it made her wet.

"Isn't it, honey?" he whispered in her ear.

"Liar!" she heard Sly and Slick yell in unison as she vanished in Wicked's arms.

Chapter Three

"I love it. It's so different." They sat on the sofa in his living room and Lori leaned against his shoulder, admiring the ring. "It looks like two rings but it doesn't come apart." She twisted the bands. "You're the son of Satan. Are you sure you want to *marry* me?" Marci and Waverly weren't married and they never talked about it either.

"It does, and yes." Wicked had fashioned it himself with blood-red jewels circling the larger band. The narrower ring had a deep claret patina and tiny crimson stars, barely visible to the human eye, decorated the stone. "It's as beautiful and different as you are." And it could only be taken apart if he gave the command.

"Wicked?"

"Hmm?"

"Do we need a safe word?"

"Honey, I'm never leaving your mind. I'll always know when you want me to stop."

"I miss being in your head."

"I'm glad you're not." Lucifer had given her the power. Wicked reversed it and was surprised it held so far. Allowing Lori to see her death in his mind would cause her so much pain he didn't even want to think about it. Josette had been right. His father had spared him -- at least for now. Didn't matter, he had no intention of killing Lori, and if anyone else did, they'd die a thousand deaths in everlasting fire. Wicked would personally see to it.

"Why?"

"Lori, do you understand I am next in line to reign in Hell? Do you know what that means?"

"Yes."

"I never want you to witness what I will do."

"But I know…"

"No, you don't. I will kill people, and do it in the most painful of ways. I will bring about disasters that maim and cripple thousands." She must understand what she was getting herself into, though escaping him now was out of the question. "They will suffer forever in Hell."

"Only bad people."

"Some I will make bad, Lori, just so they go to Hell." *Like I'm making you bad.* Telling her why he planned to marry her wasn't going to happen in this lifetime or any other. "Trust me on this."

A deep sigh rushed past her lips. "How will you ever be able to -- to, well, you're very possessive by nature and I've always wanted…"

"You want to involve another man when we have sex."

"You're not angry?"

"About enjoying sex? Lori, I've been in your mind for months and I've known this."

"Being what you are, can you handle that? Marcia and Wave said…"

"Honey, I'm not Sly, or Slick." He reached for her hand and pulled it to his crotch. "Does this answer your question?" He was so damn hard, if Lori bumped him wrong, his dick would break. "Take the outer band off and give it to me."

"No, I want to wear them both."

Shit! Think, think. Wicked wasn't versed in all the rules of engagements and marriages, hell, he'd never thought he'd be taking vows of any kind other than to deliver pain and death. Slick and his damn idea. "Isn't there something about bad luck if you wear the wedding band before the actual ceremony?"

"Oh, you're right, but how…" She pulled and the thinner ring slipped right off. Lori handed it to him. "Don't lose it."

"Never." He placed the ring on the coffee table beside the chair. Their clothes were gone in the blink of an eye, and he pulled her up to straddle his lap. "Damn, I want you, and I've got a surprise." Her eyes were instantly covered by a dark red piece of silk. "Imagination can be a delicious aphrodisiac."

"Mmm, I like not knowing… Wicked!" Lori jerked against his chest. "Who is it?"

"Do you want to see him?"

"No." She shook her head. "Not yet." Her breathing became erratic. "I want to feel him."

The man's dick bumped her shoulder blades and he grinned. "Can I taste her?" He hefted a cock as large and as perfect as Wicked's. "Shit, she's got a beautiful ass."

"You think?" Wicked grinned. The man's dark hair was the exact length as his and his skin carried the same dark tan. Stomach muscles bunched with as much anticipation as Wick's did. He licked his lips, and said, "You can taste her." His blue eyes darkened with lust.

"What's his name?"

"Fallin." Wicked tweaked her nipples hard. "He wants to eat my pussy."

"Yes, oh yes."

Wicked turned her in his arms, spread her legs over his thighs, and lifted her arms. "Keep your arms up." He watched over her shoulder as the man jerked his dick, pulling drops of liquid from the slit. "You're shaking, honey."

"I can't believe I'm going to have sex with two men."

Fallin dropped to his knees and leaned forward. When his tongue swiped her cunt, Lori pressed her back into his chest. "You like his tongue?"

"Unnhhh, yes, Wicked, yes."

"Lick her good, Fallin, fuck her with your tongue."

Lori's hips rolled and jutted back and forth in his crotch. Cream dripped from her and slid between his thighs. Wicked could ease into her pussy if he angled his hips right. Not yet. He reached around and took her nipples in his fingers. He pinched and pulled them, making her cry out, "Harder, let me feel it."

He twisted the buds until she moaned. "Damn, honey, work that big ass." She pushed against his cock each time Fallin stabbed inside her. "Make her come." He rubbed her nipples with his palm and flicked them with his thumbs. Leaving one breast unattended, he grabbed one of Lori's arms and drew it down shoving her hand to the back of Fallin's head. He covered it with his and together they urged the man back and forth between her thighs. "Damn, that looks good, baby."

"Mmm, you like watching him eat my pussy?"

"Who's pussy is it?'

"Yours, Wicked, it's yours."

"That's right, honey, it's mine."

"Ooh… ooh…"

"Come for us, we'll make it happen again."

"Oh, shit… ahh, coming, Wick, I'm coming."

She pushed back in his crotch and the movement took him to the edge. "Fuck, stop, stop. Get up." Fallin stood facing them with the tip of his glistening cock bobbing in Lori's face. "His cock is right in front of you honey, suck it while I fuck my pussy." She leaned forward and captured Fallin's cock in her mouth as she gripped his with both hands. "Hell, yeah, honey, suck his dick." Wicked spanned her waist with his hands and lifted her hips a little. She was so wet, his cock slipped right into her cunt. "Aww, that's good."

He jammed in and out, while she swallowed the man's penis over and over. When Fallin began to moan, Wicked also stood on the verge of ejaculating a load of cum into Lori's vagina. "Take my cum, swallow his." He thrust up once, twice, and sent a stream of semen into her pussy just as Fallin filled her mouth. "Fuck, yeah!" Fallin pumped in her mouth repeatedly, giving her every inch, and every drop.

"Ahh, shit!" Fallin bellowed, shoving his dick in and out of her mouth, filling it with cream.

Lori's head bobbed up and down as she gyrated her butt in Wicked's crotch, taking everything he wanted her to have. "Get it, baby, come again, come all over my cock."

"Now, now… yes, ooh!" She whimpered.

"Damn, Lori, baby, you're fucking good."

Her head fell back on his chest, and she whispered, "Wicked good."

"We can have Fallin anytime you want."

"Are you sure?"

"Yes." Wicked twisted her head to face him. "Was it everything you thought it would be?"

"It was as if -- he tasted so much like you."

"I like that you remember my taste."

"I like how you taste." A grin curved her lips. "When can I have more?"

"Greedy." He kissed her, and nipped her bottom lip. "And sweet. Tomorrow is another day, you can taste me then." He stole the drop of blood resting on her swollen lip.

She nestled into the curve of his neck, placing a kiss there that sent his blood soaring. "I want to try so many things with you."

"Sex is wonderful with the right person."

"Or persons."

"Yeah, that too. Tell Fallin thank you."

Lori reached to remove the blindfold. "Thank you," she murmured stifling a yawn with the back of her hand. "Hey, where'd he go?"

"You need to rest. He'll be there when you want him again."

When her breathing evened out and Wicked knew she slept, he picked the wedding band up from the table and looked through the circle. "Wicked good."

* * *

"Josette wants to get to know you."

"I just popped home for lunch, I'm not sure I have time." Lori sucked in a lungful of air as she watched the pretty blonde woman Waverly called Josette fade in and out of view. Did she want to go to Hell and visit Wicked's father? After talking with the women on the island, she had to admit she was curious; however, curiosity could be an extreme troublemaker at the best of times, and right now wasn't a good time. She couldn't care less if his mother or father approved, she intended to marry Wicked whether they liked it or not. "Waverly, I'm not sure I should go without Wicked."

The woman in front of her rolled her eyes. "Do you do everything he says?"

"He hasn't said I couldn't go, it's just that…"

The ghostly woman spoke. "There is little time before he will know your thoughts. I cannot hold my powers on Earth long since I shouldn't have left Hell."

She eyed the woman. "You will not change my mind."

"I don't intend to."

Swept along with Waverly, Lori flew into an ice-cold vortex of air. When she landed on her feet and caught her breath, she opened her eyes and glanced around. She thought she'd be in Hell. "What happened?"

Wave laughed. "Trust me, we're in the devil's domain."

"But it's not hot and -- and ugly."

"Lucifer enjoys worldly comforts." Josette grinned at her. "Just don't stray toward those big doors in the back." Lori eyed the beautiful woman with interest. She no longer appeared ghostly. How had she managed to stay at Satan's side for so long? And bear him sons? "It's where the lost souls burn forever."

Lori peered around the room. "Where is he?"

Josette flipped her hand through the air. "Who knows, off torturing someone maybe. Have a seat, I thought we should talk, get to know one another."

"I love Wicked, there's really nothing else to tell."

"Oh come, we're all women here, there is always something else to tell."

Waverly had taken a seat and now flipped idly through a book. Lori wished Marci hadn't been busy, she'd feel much more comfortable than she did with Wave who she hadn't known as long. For all the goodness she supposedly embodied, Lori felt darkness in her. "I'm not sure what you want to know."

"How does it feel to have two lovers pay such wonderful attention to you at the same time?"

"How did you know?"

"Down here I can read your mind." She glared at Lori. "Wicked has blocked me outside of these chambers."

"What the hell?" Wave tossed the book aside. "Wicked-- *Wicked* -- let you have sex with someone else?"

"I only sucked his cock."

"Wow!" Waverly looked at her as if she had two heads.

"Lucifer would be surprised at how worldly our eldest has become, and he talks of marriage too?"

This woman was devious. She knew from conversations with Marcia, Josette wanted her sons to have heavenly ties and she had done everything in her power to make that happen. She lost Wicked to his father but, evidently, she hadn't given up yet. "I wonder how surprised he'd be to know you were above."

"Touché." She smiled. "I think we shall get along fine."

"Not that I want to but, dang, how did you get Wicked to let another man touch what belongs to him?" Obviously, Waverly had more to say.

At this point, Lori didn't mind telling them. Maybe it was the atmosphere. It freed her from normal restraints. "Sex is just that -- sex. Wicked understands my appetite for enjoying it in every way." She tilted her head. "It doesn't always have to be soft and emotional. Sex can be good when you use all your senses, including pain."

"Shoot, Lori, you are full of surprises."

"So is Wick, and I like it."

Wave chuckled. "Seems he may have truly met his match."

"What do you mean?"

"He teases his brothers about limiting themselves and playing safe."

"Life is too short not to be enjoyed to the fullest."

Josette peered at Lori. "It is good to know you recognize living isn't forever." She glanced at the doors toward the back. "My sons don't share anything they consider theirs, which means something is amiss." Josette nibbled a fingernail. "You know what? Waverly and Marcia should get married too."

"Why haven't you?" she asked Waverly. Lori wondered if Josette and Satan had been married, or were they only eternal lovers. "Did you marry Lucifer?"

"In our own way. It was never sanctified in a church and it would not have mattered. His love of Him," she looked up, "precluded his ever giving more than he did. Oh, he loves me, but I will always be second-best."

"How did you do it?"

"We said vows to each other on a beach, and as far as I'm concerned, we are married." Love mixed with pain darkened Josette's blue eyes.

Never in a million years would Lori settle for what she had. It served to give her some insight into the woman who was Wicked's mother. What she had lived with would make a normal woman bitter, hateful, hell, probably even mad.

"It remains to be seen if you will marry. My youngest sons cannot stay long in church. Wicked would burn within minutes."

Lori's heart flip-flopped against her rib cage. She hadn't thought about that. Had Wicked known? Was he playing a terrible joke on her? *Damn it.*

The smile lighting his mother's face was beatific. "Don't worry, if anyone can figure it out and pull it off, it's my son, Wicked. He has every devious trait possessed by the devil himself." She again glanced at the gates of Hell. "You both must go. We will talk again."

The swirl of wind picked up quickly and she didn't have time to catch her breath. Opening her eyes, Lori felt disoriented. She found herself in Wick's bed, not in her living room where Josette had visited. Work would have to wait. Angry, she jumped up and paced. "How dare he promise marriage?" She idly spun the engagement ring on her finger and tried to pull it off. The band wouldn't budge. "Bastard."

* * *

"So what the hell are we going to do?"

Sly looked so damn serious, Wicked forgot about not feeling Lori's presence when he left to talk to his brothers. She'd said she had to go to work, and that was something they'd have to discuss. His woman leaving each morning for a job did not suit him at all. He would provide everything she needed. "I guess you're getting married too." He looked across the water of Slick's little island and thought about creating something similar for Lori so they'd have a quiet place to spend their honeymoon, a place where no one could bother them, not even his father. He chuckled as he thought about it -- the sons of Satan married.

"Wave wants a white wedding."

"Marci, when she gets wind of this, will want the same."

"Where's she been she doesn't know yet?" Wick whistled. "Slick, do not tell me Marci still goes to work every day?"

"I can't stop her, man, she likes working."

"You need to put an end to it."

"What would you have me do, Wick, spank her?"

"She might like it."

"Do *not* tell me you beat Lori?"

"I tap her big ass with love, my brother." Wicked grinned. "Lori is special. She likes it."

Sly sighed. "Can we stick to the subject? Wick's deviant sex life is disgusting."

"Screw you, and what color they wear isn't important. It's a good thing it won't be held in Hell… son-of-a-bitch!" Wicked stared at both brothers.

"Damn." Slick slapped his thigh. "I forgot about that."

"What?"

"Sly, you're slipping if you don't see what's in our minds."

"Little brother did an awesome job of shielding his island from the parents after you sent the women here alone, so I thought we'd talk out loud for a change."

Slick grinned. "Just used big brother's heated bubble, figured if it kept mom out, it might work with Pops."

"Ah, that reminds me, I have sort of a wedding gift for the two of you." He rubbed his hands together and opened them. Each held a ring similar to the smaller band he'd given to Lori. "Hold out your hands." Before placing the circle in their palms, he let a talon sprout from his fingertip and scratched them. "Don't ever lose it."

"Shit, man, that hurt like hell." Slick turned his over and over looking at it.

"Beautiful." Sly gazed at him. "Wick, it's hard reading you anymore."

"Maybe I don't want you to."

"You're more and more like him every day." Shaking his head, Sly added, "Anyway, what did Slick forget?"

"A slight problem regarding the three of us walking into church." Wicked could tell something troubled Sly. He did grow stronger with each passing day, and he rooted around in his brother's head without guilt. What he saw pissed him off a little. He'd forgotten how women chatter when they get together. When would his brother divulge the information he'd gleaned from his woman? Come to think of it, when did she visit with Waverly, and why hadn't Wicked picked the information up from Lori? *What the fuck!*

"Guess that ends that." Sly kicked at the sand.

All three watched the waves move back and forth against the shoreline until Slick, in his unabashed way, broached the other issue. "How the hell did you let Lori suck someone else's dick?" He shook his head. "That's just nasty, man."

"I suppose you culled that from Sly's head?" He didn't care about his brothers knowing his sexual proclivities, hell, they should loosen up a bit in that area. What he cared about is how he did it. If his father got wind of the situation, more than hell could break loose. Josette would also be in hot water herself with the powers above. Eventually, it would come to light, but there was no need for anyone to know right now. "Remember when I told Sly he should try dipping his dick in something exciting now and then?"

"Yeah, in the club the night he fell for Waverly."

"Uh-huh, same night I said you were a sick motherfucker." Sly peered at him.

"Well, I still am." Wicked laughed as he shimmered out of view.

Now, to find out why he missed *anything* Lori thought.

Chapter Four

Lori had gone home after she waited much too long for Wicked to return from wherever he was. Probably cavorting with his brothers. She had known the three of them would be inseparable, even thought she could handle it. Now she wasn't so sure. They'd already popped in unannounced once, interrupting an intimate moment.

She wasn't very surprised when the heat in her living room heralded Wicked's arrival. Lori had expected him.

"Why are you here?"

"It's where I live, Wick." She filled her head with all kinds of nonsensical bullshit in an effort to keep him from finding out where she'd been, and what she discovered.

"Honey, you live with me now." He snapped his fingers and every piece of furniture vanished.

"How dare you."

"I prefer you let me know the next time you wish to visit my mother. I'll take you myself. And as for marrying you, I will."

"What if I don't want to marry you?"

"Say it, and I'll never mention it again." He walked over and curled a strand of her hair around his finger. "It will make you no less mine."

"What if I don't want to be yours?"

"I'm sure you know that time is long past."

"Why didn't you tell me we couldn't marry in a church?"

"Is that what this is about?"

"No. It's about not being sure I can live with you and your brothers, and every fucking body else you call family climbing willy-nilly in my head."

"It will never happen again." His eyes blinked back and forth to red a lot lately.

"Just like that."

"Just like that."

"Even your father?"

"Well, he's a little like the man above when it comes to gathering information from the minds of those he chooses to. But I think, also like Him, Lucifer has other things to worry about besides crawling around in your head."

"So he might be able to?"

"He will."

"I guess I can deal with that."

"I want to fuck you."

"Wicked?" Her panties grew wet thinking about having him. Her ardor dampened only by the fact his mother knew what Lori did with her son.

"I don't give a shit what she knows we do, she'll never hear it or see it when we're together, babe. Not even my brothers will know what we do unless we tell."

"They won't pop in again?"

"Unless their need of me is dire, no."

"What constitutes dire?" He kissed her and when his tongue entered her mouth, tangled with hers, Lori sighed and gave in to what he wanted. For now. He lashed the inside of her mouth, touched places, tasted parts no one else ever would. He was sweet, hot, and intense as he delved back and forth in her mouth. She circled his waist with her arms, held him close, didn't want to let him go. When he pulled back and stared at her with beautiful blue eyes, her knees grew weak.

"They will not interrupt us again."

"What?" His kiss seared her soul, made her forget what she had asked.

He grinned. "For you, Lori, I will consider only the end of the universe dire."

"Oh." Her thoughts blazed with ideas of things she wanted him to do to her, those she wanted to do to him. Was it important that she be his wife in the eyes of Go…

"Shh." He pressed two fingers to her lips. "It's important to me to make you my wife."

Heat enveloped her, and when she opened her eyes, she lay naked on Wicked's bed. "You have to warn me when you're going to whisk me through the atmosphere."

"Afraid I may drop you?"

"What would happen if you did?"

"I would stop the world from spinning and catch you."

"You can do that?"

"Yes." His mouth covered hers again.

This time, he seemed intent on making Lori know she belonged to him, heart and soul. His skin burned against hers. When Wick stopped kissing her, his tongue left a trail of fire as he moved to her breasts. He captured one nipple and sucked it until it hurt. Leaving it, he pulled the other into his mouth and treated it the same. His teeth bit into her breasts and he lapped the trickle of blood away. Lori knew the marks wouldn't fade unless he wanted them too. It made her happy to know when he was gone, she'd have something to look at and remember until he returned.

When her arms stretched above her head, and silken material wrapped her wrists and locked them to the head of the bed, Lori knew he was in her mind.

"Yes," she whispered. Her legs spread apart and her ankles were bound to the lower posts.

"You can't touch me, or stop me, Lori." He rose on his knees between her thighs. "How does that make you feel?"

"You already know."

"Say it, baby, let me hear it."

"I want you to make me squirm and struggle to touch you."

He leaned into her neck, licked her pulse and then he bit her there and took more blood from the small wound. He licked her neck, along her collarbone, and down to her breasts. The sensation made her pull at the bindings anchoring her to the four corners.

"Unnhhh, damn you." She wanted to rake her fingernails down his back, dig them into his buttocks.

"You will, baby, soon you will."

The thrill of not knowing what he would do next, her inability to prevent it, sent shivers throughout her body. "Please, please, Wicked." He reached her nether lips with his tongue, and Lori damn near fainted when he bit her labia softly before he licked and kissed her there. "Oooh," she cried.

"You can lift that ass, honey, I know you can. Shove your cunt in my mouth." She hiked her hips as high as possible, and Wick rewarded her by thrusting his tongue deep inside. He stroked in, out, and then swirled his tongue, taking everything he wanted.

"More, lover, I need more."

When he rose above her, she gulped air at the sight of his blue eyes fading to red and back again. "Are you afraid?"

"You won't hurt me, you'll never hurt me."

He squatted over her and used his hand to push the tip of his cock into her mouth. Lori raised her head up and down taking him as deep as possible. She used her tongue to lave the cap and lick the tender underside.

"Shit, you suck my cock good, babe." He stroked in her mouth faster, sending spurts of cream down her throat. "Enough. I want to fuck my pussy." Kneeling between her legs, he touched her, eased fingers through her creases. Using his thumb, he prodded her clit. "Hot and wet," he murmured.

Lori bucked off the bed when he started to tap her there. First it was soft and slow, then he swatted her harder, measuring each moment just long enough to allow her ass to hit the bed. Then he made her rise again. "Ahh, you like that." He continued to strike her, never going beyond pleasurable pain. When she began to pull the binds so much her wrists ached, they were suddenly gone. "Now I'm going to fuck you."

* * *

Wicked's dick was so hard and swollen, he thought he might hurt her if he shoved into her cunt the way he wanted to. He hovered over Lori and rubbed his length back and forth through the wetness gathered in her creases. "Damn, I want you."

"Take me, hard, I don't want soft and easy, Wicked." She shoved her hips high and at just the right angle to draw his cock inside her vagina. Her fingers clawed his ass, pulling him deeper. "Unnhhh, yes... *yes!*" she yelled.

Slow thrusts at first, then he moved in and out faster, harder. In minutes, he was ready to shoot a stream of cum into her pussy so he stopped and withdrew. But he didn't want it to end. "Turn over." He grasped her around the waist, pulled her back and let her feel his engorged dick. "You're going to take all of me." Wicked let the tip of his penis touch her labia, teasing Lori until she bumped her ass back and forth against his crotch.

"Wicked, don't... don't let me go."

"Not in a million years." He used his hands at her waist to hold her still before he jammed every inch inside her. He pulled out and stroked in again and again. Her vagina convulsed around his thickness, pulling, holding it. "Squeeze my cock, honey, squeeze it tight." He rode her long and hard, taking her to the edge.

"Wicked!"

"Talk to me, Lori, tell me what you want."

"Keep giving me your cock, *my* cock."

"That's what I wanted to hear." He pummeled her again, taking everything she offered. "It's yours, all yours."

"Let me come, *make* me come."

"I want to feel your cream surround my dick." He moved faster in her pussy, enjoying feeling her ass slam into him with each stroke. Reaching the point of no return, he groaned as his orgasm crested and shot out, filling her with his seed. "Yeah... fuck, yeah!"

She cried, "Wicked!" And let her own release spring free, sending liquid pulsing from her cunt. "Oh, God."

"No, baby," he said as the room shook around them and he collapsed on her back. "Say *my* name, say Wicked. I want to hear it to Hell and back." His father picked the worst time to call him. Damn, he was a real son-of-a-bitch. "Fuck me to tears."

He felt their bodies hurtling toward Hell, and could do nothing to stop it. What was Satan up to dragging him below? It wasn't time for... shit, the time would be when his father said it was time. Wicked had to make sure he didn't tell Lori anything.

"Lori, trust me, and do everything I say."

"Well, well, well." Satan stood tall beside his throne in full hellacious regalia. His horns were black as onyx, the long tail lay coiled at his hooves and his talons tapped the thick, gnarled wood encrusted with gemstones. None of them rivaled the fire in his eyes.

Wick covered Lori's body in a long red robe. "Father." No need in saying anything to give him ammo to fire back. "This is Lori." He looked over his shoulder to find her mouth open. "Yeah, he tends to have that affect on women." He glared back at the devil. "Why are we here?"

"I don't know, maybe I wanted to meet Lori."

"Lucifer, be kind, she is a guest." Josette appeared wearing royal blue this time. How she got away without dressing in red or black perplexed him. "Nice to see you, Lori."

Wicked smiled. "Shouldn't you add *again*, Mother?"

"Oh, our visit was really very short."

"And how'd she get here without you leaving?"

"Tsk, just a small thing."

He watched his father eye Josette. He didn't know. Seemed someone above maneuvered the meeting and caused Pops to miss it.

His head swiveled in Wicked's direction. "Don't push it, son, I'd hate to scare your bride-to-be."

"How'd you find out, *Father*?"

Satan laughed, jarring everything in the room, and he heard Lori gasp. "Why does your marrying me anger him?"

"It doesn't."

"He's right, I'm not angry at all. Why don't you tell us, Wicked, how you plan to pull this off since you cannot walk into a place of worship?"

"I can marry her anywhere."

"Who will perform the ceremony if your plan is to work?"

That would be the hard part -- getting a holy man to perform the ceremony. Being in close proximity of a priest, reverend, or any man or woman ensconced in the church would cause their hellacious side to surface. Sly and Slick might make it for a very, very short time, thanks to Josette. Wicked wouldn't last a minute in their presence.

"What's he talking about, what plan?"

"We'll talk about it later."

Lori stepped in front of him and glared. "I want to know now."

"You boys sure know how to pick women. They all seem to have balls." Satan chuckled. "Tell her about your and your brothers' plan."

Wicked closed his eyes and opened his mind to Sly and Slick. Before his father could react, Lori vanished from the room.

The devil never uttered a word. He just watched Wicked.

Refusing to rise to his bait, Wick stood his ground and bided time. The air grew hot and menacing, but that only lasted for a few seconds before his father snapped his fingers and Wicked found himself back in his apartment.

Lori and his brothers were nowhere in sight. "Goddamn it."

The building rocked violently on its foundation, and the windows rattled in their frames. He thought briefly about how the demons in the building must feel each time his father vented his wrath on his sons or their women. They probably quaked in their fancy human shoes wondering if they were going to be transported back through the gates of Hell.

You have changed nothing, my son.

"The hell I haven't."

* * *

"I'm going to scratch the eyes out of the next bastard who pulls me through space. Got it?" She glared at Wick's brothers.

Slick had the decency to look apologetic. "We had no choice. Wicked commanded it."

"So, you answer to him and not your father?"

"Both, really, but he's our sibling. We can't deny him."

Sly sat on the sand. "Slick, would it be too much to ask that you fashion a home here sometime in the... oh, next few minutes? I'm sick and tired of sitting in the sand and ruining my slacks."

"So fabricate more. I can't build anything without Marci approving it."

"For crying out loud." Sly waved his arms and a large cabin appeared inside the tree line.

"Hey, fucker, this is my place, get your own." The house made a crashing noise as it tumbled in on itself.

"Hello!"

"Sorry, Lori."

"How long will we be here?"

"Until Wick says so."

She watched as Sly brushed imaginary sand from his pants, and Slick tossed stones into the water.

"I'm not staying here another minute."

Sly glanced at her. "How do you presume to leave? I don't think Slick's little island is listed on any shipping routes."

"Smart-ass." He was right. Lori had no power whatsoever, so she was stuck. Damn it to hell. What plan had Satan spoken about that caused Wicked to seem evasive? The devil wasn't exactly thrilled about their upcoming nuptials, but she doubted it was wedding plans. Surely, though, it had something to do with the wedding.

And there was the odd look Wick's father gave Josette when he found out she'd left Hell, even briefly. "Why is your mother banned to Hell?"

Marci had told Lori after leaving her sons with their father, Josette had been given solace in Heaven.

"Because she meddled in Slick's affair with Marcia." Sly had removed his shoes and socks and he pushed his toes into the sand.

"What?" How could their father hold her prisoner because she did something that probably helped her son?

"Look, Lori, we won't be here long. These are questions you should ask Wicked."

"I can tell her if I want."

"Go right ahead, Slick." Sly pulled a bunch of palm fronds from behind him and placed them so he could lie back. "It's your story."

"Mom stole Marci from me, and Father made a deal with Him." He looked skyward.

"He can do that?" That revelation shocked her.

Slick looked at her as if she was nuts. "You do know Father was his favorite until he created humans?"

"I know why the devil was cast into Hell."

"Considering everything, he's a wonderful father." He pushed rocks through the sand with the toes of his shoes. "For intervening on my behalf, he had to allow Mother to reside in Hell for thirteen moons." He shrugged and walked to the edge of the water.

Lori was tired of standing. Using Sly's idea, she gathered some fronds and placed them in the sand before she sat down. She glanced at Sly who appeared asleep. "Why would being with the woman he loves be punishment?"

"Mother can be a bitch sometimes." Sly didn't open his eyes. "Their lives are complicated. I'm sure one day Josette will tell you all about it."

The next thought that entered her mind, depressed Lori. Could Wicked possibly love someone more than her, so much more he would let her go. Maybe his father? "How can Satan love God more than Josette after what he did? I mean, he threw him out of Heaven."

Sly sat straight up. "Shit."

The largest wave she'd ever seen, even bigger than the one the last time she was here, rushed toward them. Holy hell, there was no way they could escape it.

"Hope you didn't mean the shit about scratching eyes out because we're leaving here." Sly bundled her in his arms and they vanished.

Chapter Five

Wicked sat and plucked notes on his guitar with one finger. Lori was angry, and he'd have to tell her sooner or later. For the first time ever, he wanted to let the music out, hear it live. Hooking a foot behind a rung of the stool, he began to play. Steve Vai's *Tender Surrender* filled the air and echoed from the walls, glass, and high ceiling. Controlled, beautiful, and though melancholy in parts, it held hope, and right now, Wicked needed to feel hopeful.

What he'd done would anger his father and his mother; still, he had no choice. Having Lori at his side meant more than anything else in the world. Unlike his father, he could not, *would not*, let his true love disappear from his life for even a single day. Making Lori understand was not going to be easy, yet, somehow he'd do it.

His fingers pulled every note and sound from the guitar. Closing his eyes he could see Lori. He sniffed the air, drew her scent into his lungs with every breath. "I will have her, Father, I must." The chords of music he elicited from the instrument smothered the words he whispered into the air.

"Wicked?"

He spun to see Lori watching him with tears in her eyes. His brothers left quietly.

"Come here, honey." He finished the final notes of the song, and sighed.

She walked over and stood beside him. "That was beautiful." She touched his cheek. "You need to tell me everything."

"I will." He strummed a few discordant strings and stared at her before he set the guitar against the amp. "Lori, as long as you live, you cannot join me in Hell."

"You can stay here."

"No, I can't, honey, I'll spend every spare moment at my father's side."

"Why?"

"Because I am firstborn."

"Is there something else?"

"Yes."

"Tell me."

"Do you want the truth?" He pulled her hand to his mouth and kissed her palm before releasing it. "Be very sure before you answer."

Lori stared out the window. Idly, and probably unaware of it, she twisted the ring on her finger. Minutes passed and he waited. When she gazed at him, he heard the answer in her mind before it left her lips. "Yes."

"To live with me forever, you must die."

"Because you will one day rule in the devil's place?"

"My father's reign is eternal, but if he has need of me, if he doesn't want to leave Hell, I will do whatever he asks."

"No matter what?"

He stroked her cheek with a finger. "You mean more than anything to me, but I am what I am. Wanting you as I do will not change that."

"If I say no?"

This was what he was afraid of. Lori couldn't say no -- not now. "You no longer have that choice."

"What?"

"Lori, I will take your life."

Her head shook as she glared at him. "No... no, it's not true."

"It is." Wicked's heart, cold and vile as it was, broke in two, because he now knew he'd be the one to do just as his father had said he would. Watching her eyes, tuning in to the chaos in her mind, tore at him, yet he would have it no other way. Lori wanted the truth. Wicked realized something else, something that brought tears to his eyes. Through all the evil he had done on his own, and that which he would do in the name of his father, he had fallen in love with the woman who stared at him with hurt and hysteria in her blue eyes. "I love you, Lori, and I always will."

* * *

"And you would still take my life?"

"If he commands it, yes." He pulled Lori to him, kissed her hard, and continued to ravage her mouth until she got away from him.

She walked to peer out the window. "I will not live like Josette."

"You are not her."

She twisted and rested her hip on the sill. "Wicked, I am not strong enough to come second in your life."

"You will be first in almost every way."

"But if Lucifer calls you?"

"Is it not enough I will always return to you?"

"No." She nibbled a fingernail. "How did Josette break away?"

She peered at him, watched anger flare in his eyes and he didn't pretend to hide it or ignore it. "You will not leave me."

"Can you make me love you enough to stay?" Her question seemed to surprise Wicked. "Answer me."

His foot struck his guitar as he stood, sending it crashing to the floor. From the look in his eyes, the way they turned from blue to red, Lori knew he heard what she did. His father's voice echoed through her mind.

Answer her, my son.

"Yes, I could." She could have sworn tears glistened in his eyes. "Damn, you are beautiful. Every curve, every piece of your flesh so soft and desirable. We are perfect for each other." He shrugged. "Pride, it's an ugly, self-serving monster if ever there was one." Wicked's lips curled into a snarl. "Never will I beg any woman to remain at my side. *Never.*"

"You will let me go?"

"Lori, you belong to Heaven, as my mother did." He kicked the guitar and the wood splintered into pieces. "In death, and without sin, you will go to Heaven."

The building swayed and metal crunched against stone.

"I will die anyway? Why?"

"Because it is so."

"What will happen to me?"

"You'll live beyond *His* gates, out of my reach for eternity."

"But…"

"But?" He strode to Lori and pulled her into his arms. "There are no buts, you will be gone from this life either way." He kissed her as if he searched for something. His tongue swept every crevice of her mouth and punished her for not loving him enough.

Lori kissed him back. "Wicked…"

With her life in his hands, Lori still couldn't let go, not yet. Wicked was right -- they were perfect for each other. She wanted to be with him once more and give him what love she could. She trembled at the thought of dying and spending the rest of her days above without him. Was it wrong for needing to feel him move inside her, take her to…

"No, it's not wrong, honey." Wicked cut her off and he didn't try to hide the red tears coursing down his cheeks. "Fallin and I will have you once more."

* * *

Snapping his fingers brought the other man behind Lori. Both were naked and Fallin pulled her back into his arms, held her trapped there. "This is what you want; it is what I will give you." Wicked pressed his chest against her breasts and loved the feel of her skin. "Hold her for us."

"Wicked, yes," she moaned.

Fallin said, "I want to fuck her in the ass."

"Do it." He pushed his hand through her hair. "You can take him without pain." He made sure her anal passage was lubed and ready.

Wicked watched her eyes as the man entered her from behind. Lori's breath hitched in her throat when Fallin seated all the way inside. Wicked reached beneath her thighs, lifting her so he could shove his cock into her pussy. When he did, she yelled, "Wicked!"

"Yeah, baby, I'm here, I'm right here." He stroked in each time Fallin pulled out of her ass, and burying his dick had never felt so wonderful. In, out, he jammed his cock, timing it with the invasion of her ass. "Is this what you wanted, honey?"

"Oh, yes… yes… *yes!*" She swiveled her hips in his arms, took all of him, then Lori shoved back to meet Fallin's thrusts. "I need it, I need you, Wicked."

"Right now, I'm yours."

Pulling out, he edged back far enough to tap her cunt and each swat made her buck forward.

"Taste me, bite and taste all of me."

He watched as Fallin's head bent and he nipped her shoulders, leaving a trail of bloody teeth marks. Wicked drew a taut nipple into his mouth and nibbled it until she squirmed and jutted back and forth.

"Give me your cock." Puffs of air buffeted his face. "Now, Wick, now."

He nudged the broad tip into her cunt and stopped. "How much, how deep, baby?"

"All of it." She shoved forward so hard, Fallin slipped out and Wick slid in so deep his balls slapped her butt.

"Shit," Fallin swore. "Come in her pussy while I hold her."

Wicked saw the gleam in her eyes, knew what she needed. "Spank her, Fallin, spank her sweet, big ass."

When he heard the first swat land, Wicked lost it. Cum spurted copiously from his dick and filled her pussy. "Fuck... fuck... fuck!" he bellowed. "Look at his cock, Lori." Untangling her legs, he set her feet on the floor, twisted her until she faced Fallin. Wicked shoved her to the floor. "He's clean for you, honey. Let me see you suck his big dick." Lori latched onto the man's cock with vengeance. Her head bobbed back and forth until she was taking all of him deep into her throat. "Shit, that looks good."

"Damn, Wicked, her mouth is hot."

Wick bent his knees, used one hand to nudge her head back and forth, the other he used to spank her. Gently at first, and then harder. Each swat echoed around the room, making him hotter than hell as his dick banged against the top of her buttocks, so hot, he was ready to shoot another load of cum. "Shit, I'm going to come on your back." He caressed the spot on her ass cheek he knew held his handprint. "Come, honey, let it go for us."

He could hear Lori's fingers dipping in and out of her pussy while the nails of her other hand dug into Fallin's thigh. He slammed into her mind, witnessed the jubilation she felt as her orgasm gathered and plunged from her cunt into her hand. "Unnhhh," she murmured rocking back and forth, her mouth still full of cock.

"Come in her mouth, Fallin, let her taste me." Wicked leaned sideways to watch him fill her mouth. "Swallow me, take my dick down your throat." He felt every stroke the man made into Lori's mouth, his head flew back, and Wicked roared when cum ripped from Fallin into her throat. "Lori... honey... aww, hell yes!" Semen shot from his cock, covering her shoulders. "So damn beautiful."

Instantly, Fallin was gone and Wick grabbed Lori to balance her. Helping her up, he eased her ass against the windowsill.

She gazed at him and said, "Fallin is a part of you."

"Yes."

He watched as she tilted her head and smiled. "You could never let anyone else touch me."

"No, baby."

"How?"

They're coming.

He clothed Lori in a red robe. "My brothers are here. My father will arrive soon." He spun to stare at Sly and Slick. "What?"

"You bastard, I knew it." Sly smiled.

Wicked asked, "Do you have the rings?"

Slick opened his hand, and Sly followed suit. Each palm held a band. Slick stared at him. "Where did they come from?"

Wicked pulled Lori in front of him and kept his arms around her. "I caught a falling star."

"You mean…"

"Yes. The childhood story Josette told us." He grinned. "Mother cannot tell a lie."

Sly glanced at his ring. "An angel?"

"A fallen angel I captured."

"Father is not going to like this."

Laughter sounded behind them. "Why not?"

Slick pivoted to see his father dressed in human finery. He looked perplexed when he peered over his shoulder at Wicked. "What's going on?"

Satan strode to the window and looked out. "It is His universe, but he gave me this world, and anything that finds its way here comes under my domain." He clapped Wicked on the shoulder. "I needed to know you were devious enough to follow my path."

Sly grunted. "You knew he'd done this?"

"I watched him give them to you on Slick's little playground."

"Shit." Slick's shoulders sagged. "I thought I'd found a place for privacy."

The devil turned to look at his sons. "I will always find you."

A white swirl of smoke appeared and when it vanished, his mother stood rigid, fists clenched at her sides. "You had no right." She glared at Wicked.

"Don't take it so hard, Mother. Father had to have one of us wholly."

"Not like this, it's wrong." A white glow enveloped her body.

His brothers stood back.

Lucifer's lips curled into a smile as he watched Josette face Wicked.

Wicked didn't like the feeling of sadness pouring into Lori's mind. But he was held powerless. "Don't, please, don't hurt her." He watched the jagged edges of a thunderbolt appear from beneath Josette's robes.

Lori spun in his arms and gazed at him. "You will always return to me?"

He looked to his father. "Father, why?"

Satan shrugged and it was as if the world tilted. Heat blossomed in the room. Torrential rain beat against the windows, and lightning slammed into the stone of the building, rocking it on its foundation. "You are mine, and if it is her you want at your side, so be it."

Wicked could only stare at the sweat beading on Lori's face. "Honey, I will find you anywhere they send you, I will bring you back to me." He kissed her softly.

She repeated, "Will you always return to me?"

"I will always return to you."

She spun around and faced Josette. "I belong to Wicked and I have sinned in the eyes of God. I have taken two lovers inside me, and that is adultery."

"One was an angel Wicked had no right to use and fashion into a part of himself," Josette screamed. Tears poured down her face. "You have not married him in the eyes of the Lord."

The building leaned precariously and groaned as if it was a living thing.

"The man I love is the son of a fallen angel." Lori clutched Wicked's hand. "I will always be with him."

Josette reared back and tossed the bolt of lightning. Before it reached Lori, his brothers threw their rings into the air and they melded with his, the third ring. The three pieces of metal spun through the air and caught the bolt, holding it tight.

Satan snatched the rings and held them along with the imprisoned bolt. His red eyes pierced each person in the room, and came to rest on Josette. "They are our sons."

"They are sinners."

"They are part of me, thus, part of Him."

Wicked watched as tears coursed down his mother's cheeks. "Can I not have one?"

Satan walked to her. "They will always be yours, and you have me when He allows." Turning to Wicked, he smiled. "Lori belongs to you, my son."

"And she will not die?"

"When her time comes, she will."

He continued to stare at the devil. "I won't kill her with my hands."

"Hell, I made that up to see if you were truly hellacious enough to do it." He chuckled. "I invented lying."

"Shit, Father, what if I had…"

"To hell with what ifs -- He will come for her."

"I won't let her go."

"Then I suggest you follow through with your plan."

Lori looked at him. "Exactly what is this plan everyone seems to know about but me?"

Wicked lifted her and spun around. "I am firstborn and when I reign in Hell beside my father, you will be my wife and carry the name Sathariel."

Slick answered Lori's question while Wicked kissed her eyelids, her nose, and her mouth. "If you marry him in a church, since he is a son of Lucifer, you will commit a grave sin."

Lori laughed. "Is that all?"

Josette wasn't smiling. "You will live in Hell for all eternity if you do."

"Shut up, woman, you'll be languishing there at my feet where you belong." The devil opened a burning pit in the floor and dropped the rings holding the bolt of lightning. "Most likely you'll be stirring up trouble for our grandchildren." Satan took her hand. "This time if you leave, I will know it." He kissed her hard on the mouth.

"No matter." A smile lit her face. "I may yet save one for Heaven." The floor jumped up and down. "Oh, stop, Lucifer, you're so petulant."

His father glanced at him. "Just so you know, each time you utter *it will never happen again* it does not pertain to me in any way." He glanced at Sly and Slick. "Create as many islands as you see fit, none will keep me from my sons."

"Fair enough. But Lori doesn't like everyone invading her mind." Wick still held her in his arms.

"It will never happen again." Satan flipped a hand in the air. "Except for you and me."

"Wave has set her mind on a white wedding." Sly nibbled his bottom lip.

Slick punched him in the arm. "She's got Marci wanting to wear white too."

Their mother clapped her hands. "I can help plan the weddings."

Lucifer glared at her. "You will have five minutes on the next full moon." A clap of thunder rumbled overhead. "Better make that three." He shook his head. "I'd suggest no fancy vows, just 'Do you take' and 'I do' will have to suffice."

"Explain why I can't read Wick's mind anymore?" Lori glanced at Satan.

"I had nothing to do with it."

Wicked cleared his throat. "Guess that can happen again." He rested her against the sill and knew from the look on her face she was all up in his thoughts.

His father grabbed his mother by the hand and vanished into the fiery pit. Sly and Slick disappeared to their apartments.

Lori grinned at him. "So, umm, does this mean I can't be with Fallin again?"

"Oh, I think I can catch another falling star." He ran a hand through her blonde hair before swatting her on the butt. "Hell's sake, I love you."

"When do I get to see you as the devil?"

He chuckled and pinched a nipple. "Take a look in my mind."

"Oh, shit!" A grin curled her lips. "I, uh, when can we…"

"Lori, you are nasty."

"It would be so good."

"Wicked good, honey, always wicked good."

J. Hali Steele

Growl and roar -- it's okay to let the beast out.
    -- J. Hali Steele

J. Hali Steele wishes she could grow fur, wings, or fangs, so she can stay warm, fly, or just plain bite the crap out of... Well, she can't do those things but she wishes she could!

Multi-published and Amazon bestselling author of Romance in Paranormal, Fantasy, and Contemporary worlds which include ReligErotica and LGBTQ stories where humans, vampyres, shapeshifters and angels collide-they collide a lot! When J. Hali's not writing or reading, she can be found snuggled in front of the TV with a cat in her lap, and a cup of coffee.

J. Hali at Changeling: changelingpress.com/j-hali-steele-a-127

Changeling Press E-Books

More Sci-Fi, Fantasy, Paranormal, and BDSM adventures available in e-book format for immediate download at ChangelingPress.com -- Werewolves, Vampires, Dragons, Shapeshifters and more -- Erotic Tales from the edge of your imagination.

What are E-Books?

E-books, or electronic books, are books designed to be read in digital format -- on your desktop or laptop computer, notebook, tablet, Smart Phone, or any electronic e-book reader.

Where can I get Changeling Press E-Books?

Changeling Press e-books are available at ChangelingPress.com, Amazon, Apple Books, Barnes & Noble, and Kobo/Walmart.

ChangelingPress.com